I couldn't help but smile as I looked at the herbs in the pots I had blessed. Their leaves glistened in the rays of the morning sun.

They were growing well. Maybe too well. Actually, I had a feeling they were growing faster than normal.

Sei

"Yup. They'll make the soup taste better."

Albert Hawke

"Indeed, her cooking is exquisite."

Table of Contents

The Saint's Magic Power is Omnipotent

NOVEL

4

WRITTEN BY
Yuka Tachibana

ILLUSTRATED BY
Yasuyuki Syuri

Airship

Seven Seas Entertainment

Johan Valdec

The head researcher at the Research Institute of Medicinal Flora. Keeps an eye on and takes care of Sei. Friends with Albert since childhood.

Yuri Drewes

Grand magus of the Royal Magi Assembly. His only interest is in research related to magic and magical powers. Has taken a keen interest in Sei.

Jude

A researcher at the Research Institute of Medicinal Flora and in charge of teaching Sei. Caring and friendly. Frequently comes to snitch the food Sei makes.

Aira

Aira Misono, a high schooler who was summoned to another world like Sei. Studying magic at the Royal Magi Assembly.

Elizabeth Ashley

The daughter of a marquis whom Sei befriended at the library. Looks up to Sei.

Erhart Hawke

Magus of the Royal Magi Assembly and Albert's older brother. A man of few words who has common sense. Always being manipulated by Yuri.

Characters

The Saint's Magic Power is Omnipotent

Sei

Sei Takanashi, an office lady who was summoned to another world to be the Saint. She's been healing people and purging monsters, and recently has been troubled by the fact that all over the place, people have begun to worship her. Enjoys cooking and making cosmetics.

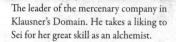

Leonhardt

The leader of the mercenary company in Klausner's Domain. He takes a liking to Sei for her great skill as an alchemist.

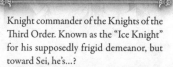

Albert Hawke

Knight commander of the Knights of the Third Order. Known as the "Ice Knight" for his supposedly frigid demeanor, but toward Sei, he's...?

The moment she got home from working overtime at the office, Sei Takanashi, an office lady in her twenties, was abruptly summoned to another world. Although Sei was summoned to be the Saint, the crown prince of the kingdom exited the room with only Aira Misono, the cute high school girl who had been summoned with Sei, leaving Sei behind.

Sei had no notion of how to return to Japan, so she soon decided to begin working at the palace's Research Institute of Medicinal Flora.

Although Sei realized that she was indeed the Saint, she concealed the truth in order to live her life as an ordinary person. However, Sei displayed tremendous magical ability, astounding everyone with her skills in potion-making, cooking, and concocting cosmetics.

Starting from the day she used one of her high-grade HP potions to save Knight Commander Albert Hawke's life, Sei performed one miracle after another. In time, rumor in the palace began to suggest that Sei Takanashi was the true Saint.

Although she was summoned by the Royal Magi Assembly to be the Saint, Sei managed to avoid being outed for some time. She took up intensive magical training under the guidance of Grand Magus Yuri Drewes, and her days were busy yet fulfilling.

Perhaps as a result of her training, or perhaps by mere coincidence, Sei performed another miracle with her gold-colored magic, strengthening suspicions that she was the Saint. However, Crown Prince Kyle denounced those suspicions, stubbornly upholding Aira as the true Saint.

However, on a monster-slaying expedition, Sei once and for all proved her Sainthood. When Knight Commander Albert Hawke was in danger, Sei called on her golden magic to instantly cleanse the black miasma producing the monsters.

As a result, Crown Prince Kyle was confined to his quarters for accusing Sei of being a false Saint. Furthermore, Aira, who had been isolated by Kyle once she arrived in the kingdom, was finally able to make friends at the academy, and with Sei. She, too, now strives for a peaceful life.

Due to the miraculous power of her golden magic, Sei was finally recognized as the true Saint. However, she still couldn't figure out how exactly to consistently call on her Saintly power.

Even so, Sei received a request to visit Klausner's Domain—the alchemist's holy land. She enjoyed the trip at first, where she became the apprentice of a master alchemist, befriended the captain of a mercenary company, and explored the possibilities of medicinal cooking.

Then, while working with her new teacher, Sei came across the memoirs of a previous Saint. Thanks to a hint in the memoirs, Sei finally figured out how to use the Saint's special powers—but the key to calling on them was so embarrassing that she couldn't tell anyone. She had to think about Knight Commander Hawke!

However, now that Sei could use the Saint's power, she could do what she had come to do: go into the forest with the knights and mercenaries, and slay the monsters within.

The Saint's*
Magic Power is
Omnipotent

THE SAINT'S MAGIC POWER IS OMNIPOTENT VOL. 4

© Yuka Tachibana, Yasuyuki Syuri 2019

First published in Japan in 2019 by
KADOKAWA CORPORATION, Tokyo.
English translation rights arranged with
KADOKAWA CORPORATION, Tokyo.

Seven Seas press and purchase enquiries can be sent to
Marketing Manager Lianne Sentar at press@gomanga.com.
Information regarding the distribution and purchase of
digital editions is available from Digital Manager CK Russell
at digital@gomanga.com.

Follow Seven Seas Entertainment online at
sevenseasentertainment.com.

TRANSLATION: Julie Goniwich
COVER DESIGN: Nicky Lim
LOGO DESIGN: George Panella
INTERIOR LAYOUT & DESIGN: Clay Gardner
COPY EDITOR: Jade Gardner
LIGHT NOVEL EDITOR: E.M. Candon
PRINT MANAGER: Rhiannon Rasmussen-Silverstein
PRODUCTION MANAGER: Lissa Pattillo
MANAGING EDITOR: Julie Davis
ASSOCIATE PUBLISHER: Adam Arnold
PUBLISHER: Jason DeAngelis

978-1-64827-296-7
Printed in Canada
First Printing: November 2021
10 9 8 7 6 5 4 3 2 1

ACT
1
Departure

I NOW UNDERSTOOD how the power of the Saint worked and could call on it whenever I pleased. Unfortunately, the secret to using it made me cringe.

I never would have guessed that the key component was thinking about Knight Commander Albert Hawke! And I had to do so *every single time* I wanted to use the magic. Was this some form of hot guy-based humiliation?!

The very thought made me scream internally, which was all I *could* do since I couldn't possibly scream externally about it. However, I could at least be grateful that I had finally been able to make some headway with my herb-growing experiments due to this discovery—especially after I had been at a standstill for such a long time.

By experiments, I mean the ones I was conducting to grow medicinal herbs that couldn't be grown without a special cultivation technique—in other words, a blessing, which I'd never seen as an agricultural prerequisite before, let me tell you. These blessings had sounded like something the Saint might be able to do, but because I had been unable to freely use my Saintly power before, my investigation had ground to a halt. However, now I was in much brighter spirits.

I'd gone to the brewery at once to tell Corinna that I wanted to explore the use of blessings. She organized everything I needed for the experiment, and we headed to the fields behind the castle together. Once everything was set up, I got to work.

I was enthusiastic about it, but the experiments themselves were actually quite simple. I blessed the soil in the pots that had been prepared for me, then planted some seeds. Nothing to it. All I had to do after that was wait to see whether the finicky plants would actually grow or not.

After I planted several varieties of seed, we were just about to make our way back to the brewery when Leo approached us. I assumed he had just happened to be passing by, but that wasn't the case. It turned out that he had actually sought me out in order to ask me to join his mercenary company.

Don't get me wrong—I liked being needed. However, I had no intentions of staying in Klausner's Domain forever, so I had to decline.

Just as I was about to reject Leo's offer, Albert showed up on the scene. I couldn't help but gasp when I saw him. He seemed different from normal, seething an aura worthy of his nickname: the Ice Knight. He stared at Leo with a frigid gaze.

You see, in his enthusiasm, Leo had grabbed my shoulders. Albert probably thought Leo and I were fighting.

Once I hastily explained the situation, the intensity of Albert's aura lessened slightly.

Then, as we were explaining *why* I wouldn't be joining the mercenaries, something seemed to occur to Leo. He stared at me in surprise. "Hold up. Are *you* the Saint?"

At his flabbergasted expression, I realized my error. I smiled awkwardly. "Oops, did I not tell you?"

"No, you sure as hell didn't! Ow!"

Indeed, I hadn't... In fact, I think I had only told him my name.

I smiled in an attempt to try to hide my mortification, but Leo's astonishment had already earned him a smack from Corinna.

"Allow me to introduce myself formally. I am Sei Takanashi, the Saint." To be clear, I was cringing on the inside as I said it. *It still feels weird to call myself that! Do I have to say I'm "the Saint" every time I introduce myself from now on? I would really rather not...*

Leo seemed to feel a bit awkward, too, since he gave a weird, "How thoughtful of you." It made Corinna shoot him an irritable look.

What was that supposed to mean?!

"So you see, the Saint cannot join your mercenary company. Was there anything else you wanted to ask her?" Albert asked, covering for the lull in our conversation.

"Uh, no..."

"Then I believe you're done here. I have business with her as well." Although Albert's expression had softened compared to how it looked when he arrived on the scene, his studiously blank face still made him appear far sterner than usual. I think he even sounded sharper.

Leo sensed the same. Although he seemed like he had something to say, he opted to back down for the moment and left us with a bow.

"Well, I should be getting back to the brewery then." Corinna started off, leaving me behind.

"Huh?" I looked at her in surprise.

Corinna turned back. "You two have something to discuss, don't you?"

I guess. "Business with her" and all that.

Corinna knew me well enough to realize I had forgotten Albert's words until that very moment. She sighed as she started back to the castle.

Albert and I now stood alone in the fields.

"Were you in the middle of something?" Albert asked as I absentmindedly watched Corinna walking away.

I looked up to find him studying the pots on the rack. His expression had become apologetic—completely different from the blank look he had worn seconds before.

"Oh, no, we just finished, actually," I assured him.

Now he looked relieved. "What are you growing? Or perhaps I needn't ask."

"Herbs."

"I knew it."

"Hey, what's that supposed to mean?" I pouted, making him laugh.

But it went without saying that between me and Corinna, who was the head alchemist of the brewery, the only things either of us would be planting were, well, herbs. But I knew he'd also pegged me for an absolute herb fanatic.

"Oh yeah, didn't you say you needed to talk to me?" I asked.

"Ah, that's right. Why don't we take this somewhere else rather than continuing to stand around here like this?"

What did he want to talk about? It couldn't be a quick question if he was suggesting we go elsewhere. In that case, it was probably better to go inside so we could relax as we talked. I followed after him at his prompting.

For some reason, Albert wanted to talk about Leo along the way. Not that I had anything much to say about the guy. The most we had interacted was saying hello when we passed each other and some small talk here and there. However, when Albert asked what *kind* of small talk, I couldn't really give an answer. "Potions, I guess?"

That made a smile cross Albert's lips.

"Oh, I met the other mercenaries recently, and they all praised my potions, too."

"Is that so?" Albert laughed at hearing this. When I asked *why* he was laughing, he smiled. "I was just remembering the time the Third Order asked the institute to make our potions as well."

Now that he mentioned it, his knights had showered me with pretty much the same reactions as the mercenaries had. Remembering that made me smile, too.

As we chatted, Albert's aura slowly returned to normal. I was relieved to not be stuck walking in silence with him while he was in an awful mood, like the one he'd been in just a few moments before. Being alone with him while he was in such a state would have been mentally taxing in the extreme.

"Leonhardt seemed eager to recruit you. Has he asked you to join his company before?"

"No, that was the first time."

"Was it now?" Albert put a hand to his chin and dropped his gaze, pondering. However, he didn't seem to come up with an answer to whatever question he had, since his brows furrowed. "Do you have any recollection of what might have prompted him?"

"You mean why he asked me to join?" Well, that I did know. "I, ah, I healed the mercenaries with my magic when they got back from their expedition the other day. I think that must be it."

"With your magic, you say?"

"Yes. At first, I was just going to give them potions from the brewery, but they said it'd be a waste, so I figured I'd just go for the magic option."

Albert's brows remained furrowed as he stared fixedly at me. Uh-oh. Was this reproach?

Uh, I guess I shouldn't have done that, huh? I slowly looked away up toward nothing in particular and heard him sigh loudly.

I'm really sorry for all the trouble I've caused! I apologized in my mind.

By then, we had arrived at our destination. Albert had brought me to the Third Order's quarters in Klausner's Domain. We entered Albert's office, and he invited me to take a seat on one of the sofas.

Oh... Has he asked me here to talk about joining an expedition then? After a short pause, I finally spoke. "So, what did you want to discuss?"

"Our plans going forward."

"You mean going on an expedition?"

"Yes. We've completed the first stage and finished our survey of the area, so I think it's about time to begin our full-scale operation."

It was finally time. As he dove into the subject, my mind switched into work mode. I reflexively straightened my posture.

I had heard reports from the knights early on, but they had continued their investigations since. Yesterday, they had finally finished their general survey. Albert proceeded to review everything they had learned about the monster situation around the domain.

To wit, there had been no change in the local monster population. There were about as many here now as there had been around the capital before I cleansed the miasma. According to locals, there were actually more monsters than there had been in the last generation. However, the mercenaries felt that in the last month or so, the number had lessened. One guy said specifically that the number of monsters had decreased since the arrival of the Third Order.

I suspected I knew what had precipitated this change.

"It sounds similar to what happened at the capital," Albert said.

"It sure does."

The only thing I could do was return his wry smile with one of my own. Merely by bringing me to Klausner's Domain, we had already begun to thin the monstrous herd.

Now the problem was determining the strength of the local fiends. They were by and large of higher rank than the ones in the capital. To be clear, the higher the rank, the stronger the monster.

Honestly, it all sounded like one of the role-playing games I had played back in Japan. In those games, the farther you got from the starting town, the stronger the monsters you encountered. Was it the same here in this world? Did monster strength correlate to distance from the capital?

Yeah, right. Jokes aside, even if we were up against the same *number* of monsters, if they were of higher rank, then we were bound to face new difficulties during these expeditions. Sure, the royal knights selected only the most promising elite warriors to join their orders, and sure, the Third Order had many such strong fighters in their ranks, but it had been years since any of them had faced monsters away from the capital.

Furthermore, the types of monsters in Klausner's Domain differed from those near the capital, so the Third Order needed to come up with new tactics to deal with them. Naturally, Albert approached everything with caution, but it seemed to me they were seeing a lot more injuries than they had during the capital expeditions. And potions had their limits, especially with the increased number of casualties. That was where magic came in.

"I'm guessing you want me to join the next expedition then?"

"Yes, and I'm sorry for that. There will be some mages with us as well, but not many people can use Healing Magic."

"It's all right, I don't mind. I was planning to participate anyway," I said. After all, my main occupation was theoretically monster slayer. Potion making was just a hobby.

"We looked into the limits of how far we can range from the domain and still return by sunset, but at present, we have yet to find the swamp. And though the monsters we've met are strong, I doubt we'll have to take on swarms of them all at once like we did back in the western forest."

"The swamp?"

"Yes, like that black swamp we found near the capital. We suspect one of those might be the cause for the increase in monsters here as well."

It made sense that we'd be looking for it, then. When we'd first arrived in Klausner's Domain, I hadn't been able to use the Saint's magic at will, so to tell the truth, I had been a bit apprehensive about what to do if we did find another one.

But things were different now. I wasn't an expert yet, but I could summon my golden magic when I had to. Now we just had to figure out where to deploy me. After all, all the monsters near the capital had disappeared when I cleansed the last miasma swamp. I was sure the problems looming over Klausner's Domain would disappear if only we could locate this one.

Never mind the fact that what I had to do in order to use this magic was extremely, shall we say, distressing.

As I had that thought, my mind blanked out a bit.

"Something the matter?" Albert asked.

"Huh?"

"Your face looks a bit red. Are you feeling all right?"

"Oh, uh, no, I'm fine!" I wildly shook my head back and forth.

I managed to somehow escape danger with these vehement declarations. No way could I tell Albert the reason for my blushing.

Only minutes after the sun rose, the brewery filled with the sound of clinking apparatuses. Sometimes I could hear the alchemists talking, but for the most part, everyone quietly focused on their work. I contributed to the quiet, making potions in silence.

It had been a few days since I talked to Albert, and tomorrow was the big day. We would finally commence our full-scale monster-slaying expedition.

Although I would be with the knights and mercenaries, that didn't mean they wouldn't need potions. Best to be prepared, you know? So we would bring potions like always. Therefore, I was busy getting them ready.

"I've heard the rumors, but you really aren't your average alchemist, are you?" an exasperated voice said from behind me, making me jump in surprise.

I turned toward the voice to find Leo looking as exasperated as he sounded. How long had he been there?

Usually whenever he came to the brewery, he announced his presence with a bang. Today, I hadn't noticed any such entrance. It seemed I had been too absorbed in my work.

I put that matter aside for now—he'd said something that concerned me. "What rumors?"

"The ones about how the new alchemist can make a ton of potions." Leo looked at the potions lining my desk. It was the same kind of look that Jude, Johan, and Corinna had all worn when they first saw how many I could make.

I felt a bit embarrassed and couldn't help but smile sheepishly. "And where did you hear about that?"

"From your friends in the brewery, of course. And my guys as well."

"Your mercenaries have been talking about me, too?"

"They come here all the time to pick up potions, don't they? One saw you making them the other day."

Had everybody in the domain seen me at work now? It wasn't like I was trying to hide or anything, yet somehow I felt like I had been caught with my hand in the cookie jar.

I smiled a bit stiffly, but Leo seemed to mistake my mood, as he was quick to bow. "Oh, my apologies. From here on out, I shall be more mindful of the manner in which I speak in your presence."

"Huh?"

"Wait, did I get it wrong?"

"What do you mean?"

"You're not thinking that I should speak to you in a way that, uh, would better befit your status as the Saint?"

"I was thinking no such thing. Please, really, talk to me like you would to anyone else. In fact, at this point, it would be way more uncomfortable if you changed it up—I mean, we've spoken casually ever since we met."

Oh boy, had I looked irritated or something? He couldn't have been more wrong. It would have been one thing if he'd been all polite with me from the beginning, but if he suddenly got all stiff after we'd already established a rapport, I'd probably just up and die. I didn't mind his informal tone, for one. For another, if Leo started humbling himself before me, I'd feel like he was trying to put some distance between us, and the thought of that just made me a bit sad.

"I see. If that's how it is, then I'll keep up like I always have," he said.

"Please do."

"To be honest, it makes things easier for me. I'm not the best with all that polite speech." Leo grinned.

His smile was infectious, making a smile spread across my face, too. While I was relieved that he wouldn't start getting weird with me, I pressed him about these so-called rumors.

According to him, the first eyewitness from his company had made a huge deal about how the new alchemist could make an unusual number of potions. The mercenary had described exactly what he had seen, but no one had believed him at first. That only made sense. The typical alchemist could only make ten mid-grade potions a day, whereas I made them one after another until vials covered every inch of my desk.

However, the mercenary insisted that he spoke truth, so the skeptics took turns coming to the brewery under the pretense of picking up more potions. That explained why it seemed like the mercenaries always sent a different guy to retrieve their order.

In any case, the first eyewitness's report was soon confirmed by his peers.

"Did you come to confirm the rumor for yourself then?" I asked.

"Uh, well, yeah."

I had already assumed as much, but for some reason, Leo got all evasive about it. Did he have something else on his mind? I looked up at him inquisitively.

Leo scratched his head before reluctantly asking, "Are these potions for the knights?"

"Yes. I already finished the batch for the mercenaries."

"I see. Wait, that's not what I—"

So he wasn't worried about that either, huh? He seemed hesitant to say anything else, so I went back to my brewing while I waited for him to speak.

"Uh, so, are you going to join the next expedition?" he finally asked, a profoundly hesitant look on his face.

"Yes, I will. That's why I came here from the capital, after all."

"You'll be with the Third Order, right?"

"Yes." I glanced up at him, wondering why he would ask that. I saw real worry in his eyes. "What's the matter?" I asked.

"Um, it's just, I was wondering if you'll be all right."

"All right?"

"During the expedition."

"Huh?"

"I know you've gone into forests for other business, but I can't help but worry."

"You mean about our military strength?"

"Uh, something like that."

I tilted my head to the side as I tried to puzzle this out. Thankfully, Leo tentatively explained his concerns, often pausing between thoughts.

He knew about my previous venture into Ghoshe

Forest, which was located to the west of the capital—he had heard rumors about that as well. He had also heard Albert talk a bit about what had happened during that expedition. Therefore, Leo knew I would be acting in a supporting role for the knights, just like an ordinary mage of the assembly.

However, the strength differential between the monsters found in Klausner's forests versus the ones in Ghoshe was nothing to sniff at. Despite my prior expedition experience, Leo was deeply concerned about my going along on the next one.

While there were fewer monsters stalking Klausner's Domain than there had been even a month ago, they were still numerous. Furthermore, their numbers had only decreased near the central city. The outlying farmlands and meadows still crawled with beasts, and the forests farther from the city hadn't seen any such decrease at all.

Usually, in this world, the monsters that appeared in forests were stronger than the ones that roamed the flatlands. Between that and the fact that all the fiends native to Klausner's Domain were stronger than the ones near the capital, Leo had a point.

All in all, Leo feared that this expedition would be much harder on me than the last one I'd joined. His worry was only natural.

"I can't make any claims, seeing as I haven't gone into the local forests yet, but I don't think we'll go straight for the heart of the forest right away. I should be fine," I assured him.

"The monsters at the heart of the forest are far stronger than those on the fringe. If you said they were heading straight into the depths, then I would've stopped them— knights or no."

"Yeah, me too!"

"Good. But if it's as you say and they're going to take it slow and see how things go... You sure you'll be okay?"

"I'm sure. Believe it or not, I'm actually pretty strong," I joked with a smile, prompting Leo to respond in kind.

"Oh yeah? You seem pretty confident about that."

To be serious, even just talking in terms of base levels, I could claim I'm stronger than anyone here. Not that I'd ever say that out loud. "In any case, although I'm going, I'll principally be there to support the combatants. I won't be out on the front lines or anything. The knights will be there to protect me."

"I see. I guess I shouldn't have worried then."

"I'm grateful for your concern, though. Thank you."

We talked a bit more before Leo went back on his way.

As you might expect from the head of a mercenary company, Leo was really good at taking care of people.

I could tell as much from the fact that he came all the way out to the brewery purely out of concern for me. And he did all that even though I wasn't part of his company.

Early the next morning, Albert and I headed for Lord Klausner's office. As I would be joining the expeditions starting that day, Lord Klausner wanted to have a formal word before we departed. While he greeted me in a noble manner, the rest of what he had to say pretty much boiled down to "Be careful out there, and come back in one piece."

Based on what Albert had told me before, we would ease our way into the forest, so I really wasn't that worried.

As we headed to the courtyard where the Third Order was gathering, we talked through our next steps. Good thing we did, too, because I just barely managed to avoid a panic-inducing scenario.

"Are we just going to assemble and head out?" I asked.

"That's right. We'll leave after I say a few words to the knights."

"Is there anything I need to do?"

"Hmm? Would you like to give a rousing speech?"

"Nope! I would much rather not."

No way could I give a speech like that in front of a ton of people. I really hated any kind of attention, honestly.

Admittedly, that had probably been a joke. I noticed Albert's shoulders quiver a bit after I turned him down. He covered his mouth with his fist and looked like he was holding back a hearty laugh.

Recently, he'd been treating me a lot like Johan did. I supposed they were childhood friends, so maybe they shared a sense of humor.

I glared at him reflexively, and Albert was unable to stop himself this time—he chuckled quietly.

When we arrived at the rendezvous point, the number of people overwhelmed me. There were way more than usual. Probably because this time the knights would be joined by the mercenaries.

However, this would be the only time we gathered en masse, as this would be the Saint's first expedition in Klausner's Domain. I was to be formally introduced. Not only that, the mercenaries would be coming along as well.

I had to pass by the mercenary company to get to the carriage that had been prepared for me, but they didn't start staring at me in wonder or anything. After all, I had my head covered with the hood of my robe, which was the same kind the other mages wore. Another mage happened to be walking near me, so I probably just looked like I was with her.

"Here." Albert proffered his hand before I got into the carriage.

I stared at it for a moment. Then I shifted my gaze up to his face to find him smiling at me in such a way that he almost seemed to sparkle.

Uh... Oh, right, he's trying to be my escort.

"Thank you." I smiled somewhat nervously as I slowly placed my fingertips on top of his palm. *Eek. I'm still really not used to this type of thing.*

I had ridden on horseback with Albert back in the capital many times, and we were close enough that we were on joking terms. I always thought I was used to being around him, but touching his hand even for reasons like this still made me nervous.

It was almost like he read my mind, because the moment I got into the carriage and started to pull my hand back, he suddenly squeezed my fingertips. It was only for a second, but it was a strong enough attack to make me blush.

I sat down in the carriage and looked back at Albert to pout at him a bit. He smiled at me as if to say "Got you!"

Guilty as charged, huh?

The doors to the carriage closed, and Albert made his way to stand with his knights, where he called them to order and laid out the day's plan. Soon after, we set off.

Things are the same as always. My cheeks still feel a bit hot, but I'm sure they'll cool down soon, right? Right now, I need to focus on the expedition, I thought as I watched the scenery go by from inside the carriage.

About an hour into the journey, Albert rode his horse over to the carriage. "Sei, it won't be long before we arrive."

I stretched my back where I sat and reached for my bag that I had set aside. Just as I finished checking through it to make sure I had my knife—in case of an emergency—and all the potions I wanted tucked inside, we arrived.

Just as he did when I climbed into the carriage, Albert came to assist me in getting out as well.

Upon my release, I was overcome with a sense of freedom and stretched with a loud groan.

"Hah. You tired?" he asked.

"No, just feeling a bit stiff from sitting for so long." Not to mention, stretching inside the carriage hadn't gotten all the kinks out. The way Albert laughed made me feel a bit self-conscious, though. "A-anyway, we're finally here! I've never been in this forest before, so I'm kind of looking forward to it."

"You mean you're looking forward to seeing what kind of herbs grow here?"

"Exactly! Ah, I mean..."

"I suspected as much. It'll be tough to keep an eye out when we're on the move, but we can look around a bit when we stop for a break. I'll accompany you."

"Oh, I couldn't possibly trouble you so."

I tried to change the subject, but it was too late.

What was that about focusing on the expedition, Sei? Ack, I let my guard down in front of him again. And is it really okay for me to get this distracted when we're about to go into the forest? Knowing myself, I'm a bit worried.

As I fretted about my own tendencies, Albert's head raised and his demeanor stiffened.

I looked up and noticed someone approaching us. "Leo?"

"Hey there!"

I'd known the mercenaries were accompanying us, but it turned out Leo was among them. Made sense to me, as he was their captain.

Albert's eyes got a funny look as Leo waved at me.

Uh, is it because he thinks Leo is acting improperly toward the Saint? While manners were important and all, I personally didn't want people to get all formal with me, so I also didn't really want Albert to make a big deal about it. I probably needed to tell him that either way.

As I glanced between the two of them, Leo turned to Albert and bowed his head slightly. "I look forward to working with you today."

"The feeling is mutual. While my knights and I conducted preliminary surveys of the area, I acknowledge that you and your men are far more familiar with the forest."

"Thank you for your kind words," said Leo. "And I look forward to working with you today as well, Lady Saint."

"Huh?" I looked at Leo in surprise. What was he calling me now?

Leo's eyes darted toward Albert for a moment.

Ah, I see... I mustered a smile. "And I look forward to working with you as well. However, I don't much care for all this pomp, so I would feel far more comfortable if you continued to treat me as you have."

Albert hesitated. "If it's as she wishes, I won't argue."

"Thank you. It shall be as you wish," Leo replied.

Leo doesn't come off as the attentive type, but he's surprisingly adept at navigating social situations. I gave him a mental thumbs up for helping smooth that moment over.

"I'll see ya later then." Leo gallantly turned on his heel.

He sure can code switch quickly. I couldn't help but smile. I glanced up at Albert, who was looking back at me with a soft expression.

"We'll take a short break before we head in," Albert said.

"All right. It looks like they're boiling water over there. Shall I make some tea for us?"

"No, I believe my retainer will prepare it. Let's enjoy a cup together."

"Yes, let's!"

While the forest was close to the city, we had traveled some distance, so it was best to rest before we actually moved out. Luckily, it turned out Albert was right—his retainer had made us some tea. Not only that, the man had set out a pair of folding stools as well.

I sat, and while Albert and I chatted, everyone else finished getting themselves ready to go. It wasn't long before I was handing my cup back to the retainer, and we quickly cleaned up our rest stop. Then, everyone followed after us as we proceeded to enter the forest.

At first glance, the vegetation in the forests of Klausner's Domain didn't look all that different from the kind found in the capital. However, upon closer inspection, I noticed all sorts of flora I hadn't seen in the capital's forests—and they grew all over the place.

"Whatcha looking at?" Leo asked as he walked next to me.

"There are some herbs I've never seen before," I said.

"Herbs? But you're not an alchemist, right?"

"I *am* a researcher at the Research Institute of Medicinal Flora."

"I thought you were supposed to be the Saint."

"I am, but I prefer to think of that as a side gig."

Leo burst out laughing. Aw, come on, I'd just told him what I wished were true!

The knights had split up into squads like they had during our expedition into Ghoshe Forest. The mercenaries had joined two of those squads, one of which was the one I had also joined. Actually, all but one of Leo's mercenaries were up ahead with the vanguard, so he was the only one with our group.

So there I was, Leo on my right and Albert on my left.

"Hey, now. Is it really okay for you to be saying that?" Leo asked quietly, nodding subtly toward Albert.

"Oh, yes, no worries." At least, I wanted to think so. I held myself back from saying anything more.

"It's fine. She's entitled to see her position how she likes," Albert said before I could.

I almost started laughing, but I didn't. Frankly, I deserve a lot of kudos for that.

After we had been walking for a bit, Leo frowned. "This is strange."

"What is?" I asked, tilting my head.

"There's a damn sight fewer monsters than I expected."

"Oh?"

The knights had said nearly the exact same thing a few times before, back in the capital. I hadn't seen the decrease personally, so I couldn't confirm, but the monster population near the capital had dwindled after the Saint Summoning Ritual. I suspected it was the same case here in Klausner's Domain.

Meanwhile, Albert looked like his own suspicions had been confirmed. "So there really are fewer then?"

"Yes. I heard your surveys encountered a minimal number as well. We are indeed seeing fewer than we had in the past," Leo replied.

"We witnessed a similar phenomenon back in the capital."

"Huh."

Leo continued to treat Albert like a noble, just like he had from the start. I guess that meant he only spoke so casually to me on account of my explicit request, which had come personally from me, the Saint. Oof, the gossipy types were bound to talk about this.

However, the conversation reminded me that in the first forest I went to, Saul Forest, which was located to the south of the capital, had been just like this. We hadn't seen any monsters at all when we went herb picking.

Notably, as one would expect from a forest said to have powerful monsters, we did run into a couple. However, the frequency of these encounters remained markedly low.

Of course, we all knew the reason for that. I just wished my two companions would stop looking at me!

The Saint's
Magic Power is
Omnipotent

ACT 2
Troublesome Things

WE PROCEEDED AT A GOOD PACE until we settled in a clearing where we took our lunch break. We ran into a few more monsters before we got there, but Leo and Albert took care of them in the blink of an eye. All I had to do after a fight was cast a quick Heal on them, so we continued at a leisurely pace.

Just like the expedition into Saul Forest, the other squads ran into more monsters than we had. For the record, the knights did feel that the local monsters were a bit tougher than the ones in Ghoshe Forest had been.

The glade where we stopped was the same place the mercenaries used when they took a break on their regular outings. As planned before we departed, all the squads had taken different paths through the forest and met up with us here around noon.

Johan banned me from cooking in public, but the majority of the people here are the knights of the Third Order. It's okay if I help them out, right? I'm here to support them with magic, after all. Yeah, I'll just blame it on magic if anyone says anything. Right. That's what I'll do. With that excuse in mind, I decided to help out by making lunch.

Leo came over while I was putting together a soup for everyone. "Whatcha doing?"

"Um, cooking." For some reason I got a sense of déjà vu.

"Cooking? But you're the Saint, aren't you?"

"That's right," I said. *So I'm the Saint, so what?*

He watched me for a while, a strange expression on his face, before he gently said, "I thought the Saint was supposed to be held in much higher regard. Shouldn't someone be waiting on you right now?"

"You think so? This is how things have always been for me."

"That's weird, though."

"Is it?"

Honestly, Leo was right—when you considered the status of the Saint in Salutania, she really was supposed to be revered and waited upon. I knew this, yet I steadfastly pretended not to. It was much more comfortable for me to be treated like the person I was. I was sure Leo had guessed this.

Plus, getting to cook was a nice change of pace. I'd had to restrain myself from doing so since I came to Klausner's Domain as the Saint—outside of that one time. Not to mention, it would have been weird for an outsider like me to keep barging into the castle kitchens. But I didn't have to worry about troubling others when preparing food during an expedition. Also, the only people around already knew what was up with me. No way could I let this chance pass me by.

"That smells amazing," said Albert as he came over, no doubt drawn by the aroma.

"Oh, Lord Hawke."

I smiled a bit as I stirred. The feeling of déjà vu was getting even stronger.

Albert took up the position opposite Leo and peered into the pot. "Is this the same soup you made for us before?"

"Yes. I asked the knights if they had any requests and a number of them asked for it."

Albert placed a hand to his forehead and hung his head as if he had a headache. "Did they now?"

Although it was the knights' request, this sort of dried meat and vegetable soup was a staple on expeditions, according to one of the retainers.

"Wait, wait, you're putting herbs in there, too?" Leo asked when I started adding herbs such as oregano and thyme.

"Yup. They'll make the soup taste better," I explained.

"Indeed. Her cooking is exquisite," Albert added.

This soup would also have the effect of increasing the natural recovery rate of one's HP, but I didn't say that. Albert also kept it mum, only mentioning the taste. However, calling my cooking *exquisite* was a bit of an over-exaggeration, if you asked me.

I finished making the soup, so next was the main dish. I turned to find the people in charge of cooking for the Third Order preparing some kind of meat. They looked to be salting it and then grilling it with an herb butter that had been prepared in advance.

What kind of meat was it though?

Wait, what? I blinked in surprise. It seemed the mercenaries had killed a boar they ran into along the way. How often did this happen? Often, it turned out. The mercenaries really were as crazy as I thought they might be.

The rest of food prep went off without a hitch, and the retainers distributed soup and meat to the knights. I couldn't really relax until I heard the chorus of delight at the taste—only then did I sigh with relief.

Even Leo raved about how delicious it all was while shoveling it into his mouth. Albert showered me with praise, a sparkling smile on his face. I was just glad they liked it.

Once we were done with lunch, we continued the expedition. But first, I cast a support spell on the knights before the squads split off again.

"Area Protection." A magic circle spread around me on the ground, and a white mist with dancing golden particles rose up from it.

That spell raised an individual's defense against both physical and magical attacks. The knights were used to it by now, but the mercenaries, who had never seen such magic before, made a big fuss. Leo was among them.

"Oh, incredible!" he exclaimed. "I definitely feel that."

"Is this the first time you've had a spell cast on you?" I asked.

"Yeah. There're hardly any mages around here, y'know, let alone any that can cast area-of-effect spells."

"Ah, that's true." It made sense when he put it that way. I had read that area-of-effect spells were more difficult for the average mage versus single-target spells.

"Not to mention, no other mage can cast a spell on this many people at once," added Albert, who was standing next to me. His tone was rather admiring.

"What? Really?"

"Indeed," he said. "By leveling up our Magic skills, we can increase the range and duration of our spells, but no one alive could match your ability."

I had a feeling Grand Magus Yuri Drewes had said as much to me before, but I had, er, completely forgotten.

If he were here right now, I bet he'd have a huge grin on his face—but he'd be feeling something else underneath. I'm scared just thinking of what would happen next. I got chills down my spine. *That was a close one. I better be more careful.*

Once I was done casting, we split up and recommenced our walk through the forest. The farther we got, the more monsters we ran into. Although they were more powerful than the ones in Ghoshe Forest, the knights dispatched them easily enough. They routed them one after another with superb tactical coordination.

Meanwhile, I was on healing duty—although I just stuck to the normal kind. But listen, the reason I didn't use my Saint's magic had *nothing* to do with who I had to think about in order to use it. Really! Albert and I had discussed whether I should use it, and we had decided I would hold the power in reserve. It had nothing to do with me feeling self-conscious, I swear!

At one point, the mercenaries at the vanguard gave the order to stop. I peeked ahead between the knights to see what the problem was and spotted an unfamiliar entity.

"Huh?"

"What is it?" Albert asked me.

"Oh, it's just that I've never seen that kind of...thing before."

"That type of monster doesn't appear near the capital. Careful—it's venomous."

Considering Klausner's Domain was known for its herbs, I supposed it wasn't that surprising to run into a monster that looked a lot like a carnivorous plant. Frankly, the way the giant sundew's spines waggled around kinda skeeved me out. Luckily, unlike all the other monsters we'd seen, this variety was rooted to the spot and couldn't move. Which was a good thing, because it probably would've grossed me out even more if it could.

Venomous, huh? Does that mean it could give someone one of those harmful status effects?

Just as I thought that, the battle began. I watched from the back line as the sundew bent its stalk back and flung itself forward. At the same time, round droplets from the tips of its spines flew at the knights. Most of them dodged, but wherever a droplet landed, I heard the sizzling sound of meat cooking—venom, then.

I was the only one surprised by the sound; everyone else kept fighting like normal.

Whenever someone got hit, they'd shout out, "I've been poisoned!" But they kept pretty calm about it. A mage would then cast a spell to heal the harmful effect.

Magic sure was incredible. The effects were gone in the blink of an eye.

The battle itself was over quickly. I cast Heal on everyone who'd been hurt, and we were once more on our way.

After that, we started running into a certain sort of monster more often—i.e., we kept running into sundews. They didn't spray their venom every time, though. I stood at the ready just in case at each battle, but my magic wasn't required again. However, I knew it could turn dangerous if I lost focus.

Soon, when I had lost count of how many sundew monsters we had fought, we ran into yet another one. It swung wide. As it did, I unleashed the magic within my body, readying the spell to cure status abnormalities. I didn't know how many people had been hit—and it would have been a pain to heal them all individually—so I went for another area-of-effect spell.

"Area Purification!"

I timed it just right. A brief jolt of surprise ran through everyone. The status effect healed the squad a split second after the venom hit them.

You guessed it, I was putting my gaming experience to good use.

Before I joined the company I had been working at, I had played a lot of multiplayer online games. In those games, we'd make parties to kill tough monsters, kind of like we were doing now. It was in those games that I had learned to study a monster's movements and to prepare time-consuming spells in advance.

As such, every time a monster used a skill that caused a status effect, I was ready to counter it. If I watched the monster's movements, I could even tell what kind of status abnormality it would cause. However, it took time for status-curing spells to go off. Therefore, to properly time my heals for right after the attack hit, I had to start matching the timing of my casts with the monster's.

Part of it was because the people I had played with had wanted their negative effects removed right away, so at some point, it had just become second nature to time my spells that way. Admittedly, if I was too slow, people would complain, so I also got good at it because the party I played with had some strict expectations.

Consequently, I started casting Area Purification whenever I saw a sundew making its move.

"Whoa! That was amazing!" Leo exclaimed in admiration.

"Brilliant as always. Is this the fruits of your training with Lord Drewes?" Albert asked.

Well, no. This wasn't something Grand Magus Yuri Drewes had taught me. But I doubted Albert would understand what I meant if I said I learned it from a game, so I just smiled a bit. "I guess you could say that. Thank you."

I had a feeling Yuri might teach me something similar someday anyway. He did seem the type to prize efficiency.

After that, we continued as planned, and my first expedition in Klausner's Domain came to an end without anything too unfortunate occurring.

My leisurely life turned pretty busy with the addition of the daily expeditions. There was a lot to be done in what little time I had. Although, I probably only thought it wasn't so bad because I'd worked at a black company before.

I definitely didn't want to think I was okay with it because I was actually a workaholic.

We set out on our expeditions in the morning, so I got potions ready for the Order to use once we returned to the castle after dinner. Stirring a pot in a dark room by candlelight made me really feel like a witch.

Once, Corinna caught me in the brewery and sounded really exasperated as she scolded me for working so late into the night.

After I finished my potions, I bathed and went to sleep. Then I'd get up early in the morning, ready myself for the expedition, and head to the herb fields to check on the pots for my blessing experiment before I had to go.

"Oh!" One day, I noticed a change in one of the pots. The flat soil had bulged a bit.

"How are they doing?" Corinna asked, coming up behind me. She also made it a daily habit to check on the experiment.

"Look! It's sprouting!"

"What?!" Corinna excitedly peered into the pot. "It really is."

"Yeah!"

We looked at each other and smiled at the same time. Unable to contain our emotion, we both let out a cheer.

I wanted to stay to examine my herbs more thoroughly. Although one had sprouted, we still didn't know whether it would grow well. Unfortunately, it was time for me to go. Corinna promised she would keep checking on it through the day. We would discuss what came next after I got back. With that, we went our separate ways. I swear I saw a skip in Corinna's step as she headed back to the brewery.

"You seem to be in a good mood today. Did something happen?" Albert asked during our lunch break.

It turned out that I was in such a good mood that I had been humming. I supposed I couldn't really comment on Corinna's excitement. I grinned. "The herbs we planted are starting to sprout."

"Are they special?"

"Yes! We didn't know if they'd take, so it's wonderful that we got them to sprout."

"I see." Albert smiled.

I probably should have given him more details, but that would have included information only Lord Klausner and Corinna knew, so I kept it to the basics.

"Did you grow these herbs back at the institute, too?" he asked.

"Uh, I don't think we have them in the capital." We grew a number of varieties at the institute, but not these. In fact, we wouldn't have been able to at all, as their cultivation required blessings. However, I couldn't tell Albert this, so I again kept it vague.

The next thing he said took me by surprise, though. "Does that mean you'll be growing new herbs when you get back then?"

Grow them at the institute? Now that he mentions it, if I blessed our fields, we might be able to cultivate these rare seeds as well. I'm still only experimenting though. But if I'm successful, I guess I'll ask Corinna what she thinks.

"Good question. I'm not sure, since we don't know if they'll thrive yet."

"You should ask Johan for help."

"Why's that?"

"He's good at nurturing plants."

"Oh, you're right."

I had forgotten that Johan could use Earth Magic. Earth Magic included spells that were useful for growing herbs, and Johan made full use of them to cultivate the institute's gardens, especially the plants said to be hard to grow. Even if the herbs that had sprouted were unable to continue growing, we might be able to manage it with Johan's help.

Whether this worked or not, I was going to make sure to ask Corinna if I could continue these experiments at the institute. As I made future plans, lunchtime came to an end.

Huh? Already? But there was no helping it.

We had decided to start our expedition close to the capital and gradually range farther away. The farther away we got, the stronger the monsters grew and the harder it became to take breaks. As a result, we started taking frequent short breaks instead of the one long one.

I've been preparing lunch in the field, but that might become difficult before long. Maybe we'll have to start bringing lunchboxes instead? I wondered absentmindedly while I finished cleaning up after myself, and then we headed off for our afternoon rounds.

"There's another one," Albert said quietly next to me when one of the knights walking in the front gave the signal.

The knights kept on high alert while we walked, but the moment we encountered a monster, the tension in the air always sharpened. I fixed my attention on the monster so I could provide support.

This plant monster looked like a tropical pitcher plant. It had tentacles, which real pitcher plants lacked, and it waggled them back and forth. It probably would have been bad if someone got caught by those tentacles, but the knights smoothly dodged them as they made their own attacks.

They soon dispatched the monster thanks to their skillful teamwork. I was relieved that no one got hurt. Their daily training really spoke for itself.

"Good job. You guys made that look easy," I said.

"Not easy enough. The monsters are only getting tougher as we go. We must remain vigilant," Albert said with a serious look. I nodded.

The knights had the advantage at present, but we had no idea when the scales might tip in the monsters' favor. As they say, carelessness is the greatest enemy. We couldn't let our guards down. The fights started to get longer, too.

"I feel like the monsters are more frequent now," I said.

"Yes. It could be that our quarry's in this direction." Albert squinted as he looked ahead.

I nodded again. He didn't say it outright, but I could guess well enough. We had experienced this same phenomenon back in Ghoshe Forest—monsters growing in strength and frequency.

The black swamp had to be close.

I didn't feel as nervous as I had back in Ghoshe, though. Perhaps it was because we knew what we expected to find, or perhaps it was because I knew how to take care of it if we did.

Those around me seemed to feel the same. Since the monsters were appearing more frequently, the knights had to be more careful than ever, but I didn't sense any especial unease from them.

Besides, if there was a swamp, all I had to do was use my Saint's magic. Thoughts about what would happen if it didn't work still flitted through my head, but I locked them away.

If I had anything to worry about it, it was the monsters we'd inevitably find around the swamp. Due to the fact that monsters spawned from its murky depths, we anticipated there would be a great number of them in its vicinity.

The high density of monsters in one space almost felt like one of those rooms in a game dungeon—the kind that are filled to the brim with enemies. At least since we were in the middle of a forest, we weren't in an enclosed space, but it would still be terribly dangerous to face a swarm like that.

Even battle-loving Grand Magus Yuri Drewes would have trouble taking on so many monsters all at once. Although, one of the reasons he would have trouble was because in a forest, he couldn't use his big, wide-ranging spells without friendly fire. I was pretty sure I had once heard him grumbling about how he just wanted to burn everything to the ground.

It wasn't until just after this that we realized the situation was far worse than we had anticipated.

As we pressed deeper into the forest, the type of monsters changed again. We saw fewer monsters that looked like carnivorous plants and more that looked like mushrooms. I say mushrooms, but most of them had those bright, poisonous colors, so it didn't once occur to me to try eating one of them.

Just as you would expect from that appearance, the mushroom monsters' attacks caused status effects. The spores they spit out poisoned and paralyzed the knights. Apparently, they could also emit spores that burned skin.

I cured the status effects each time they occurred, but we grew increasingly cautious.

How far have we gone now?

The knight at the front of the squad called for Albert's attention. Albert glanced my way, and I nodded to assure him I'd be all right. At that, he swiftly made his way up the line.

"I wonder what's wrong," I said to the mage next to me.

"It's hard to tell from here, but it doesn't seem like an emergency."

I could just hang back, but I'm curious. Maybe I'll go ask.

I peered ahead at Albert. He and a few knights at the front were deep in conversation, frowning. They didn't seem to be panicked or anything, so I figured it would be okay if I joined in.

"Has something happened?" I asked when I did.

Albert looked at me with a frown still on his face. The other knights looked similarly concerned. We definitely had some sort of problem.

"We found traces of a troublesome monster."

"Troublesome?"

"Quite."

A knight directed my attention to a fallen tree on the ground. People came into the forest to gather resources all the time, and a fallen tree wasn't that unusual. I tilted my head with a puzzled look, and the knight pointed at the spot where the tree had fallen.

Hmm? I squinted and noticed something that looked a bit shiny at the split base of the trunk. *What's that? Some kind of slug tracks?*

"What is it?" I asked.

"It's traces of a slime having a snack—they probably ate through the tree."

"A slime?!" The image of a blue, droplet-shaped monster from that famous role-playing game popped into my mind.

Since we had encountered a variety of monsters, ranging from animals to carnivorous plants and mushrooms, I might have expected a slime mold to come next but not an actual slime.

Slime mold and slimes are similar, I suppose. So maybe my guess wasn't all that off, I thought. But as I listened to Albert and the knights discuss the situation, I realized that the slimes of this world weren't anything like the adorable low-leveled monsters found in that one game series.

According to them, slimes were terribly difficult to defeat, and if at all possible, they wanted to avoid encountering any. I realized I had read something about this—physical attacks weren't very effective for dealing with this particular kind of fiend.

"Would magic work?" I asked.

"It would. Most slimes can't defend against it."

That was reminiscent of something an old gamer friend of mine had once said: "If physical attacks won't cut it, then just nuke it with magic."

I tried to hold myself back from laughing out loud at the memory.

Our squad was mostly comprised of knights. Since Albert and I could both use magic, we only had one other mage. We didn't have that many mages with us to begin with, so each squad only had one to three mages with them. Some of the knights could use magic, too, but only a handful of them. Plus—and maybe this went without saying—the knights' Magic skills weren't much compared to an actual mage's.

As such, if a squad met just one or two slimes, they could probably take them out without much trouble. However, if the slimes came one after another like the monsters had back in Ghoshe? It would get dicey, to say the least.

Although, it occurred to me that I might be able to wipe them out all at once with my Saint's magic. I still felt a tinge of apprehension. I wasn't accustomed to actually wielding the Saint's power yet, so I didn't know if I could effectively summon it up in an emergency. It was at least reckless to think I could defeat them single-handedly in my current amateurish state.

"If only magic can defeat them, then our squad formation might not be best," I said.

"Agreed. We'd probably manage a few, but if they came out in droves, we'd be in trouble."

"So should we stop here for today and head back?"

"No, let's go a bit farther in. I want to see the situation in the forest depths."

Albert seemed to share my concerns. However, after weighing the risks, he decided to prioritize surveying—under the assumption that we would withdraw the moment there were too many slimes to deal with, of course.

Indeed, as we proceeded into the forest, we ran into slimes several times. I had heard them described beforehand, and they definitely weren't as cute as the ones found in that game series. They weren't droplet-shaped

either but softer—more like a puddle of gel spread across the ground. Also, they had no eyes or mouths.

We were lucky that we didn't run into too many at once and that Albert and our squad mage were able to defeat them. I didn't participate offensively, but I did help out. The slimes also used attacks that caused status effects, just like the mushrooms did, so I diligently healed everyone who was affected.

After we defeated yet another slime, I took in our surroundings and discovered that the scenery of the forest had changed. There wasn't much grass growing beneath our feet, and I could see patches of bare earth here and there.

Was there always such little undergrowth? Is it just my imagination? I wondered.

But it wasn't just my imagination. Now that I had noticed it, it made me uneasy, and I cautiously started examining the state of the forest.

There were more withered trees in the depths. I didn't see any obvious external causes, and it seemed like there were a whole lot more dying trees than there should have been in a healthy wood.

Back in the world I came from, forests were vulnerable to acid rain. Is that what caused this, too? Nah, couldn't be...

Furthermore, the dead trees were oddly interspersed.

"Is something the matter?" Albert asked me.

"I was just thinking that something seems off about the forest here."

"You, too? I noticed the atmosphere was different."

"There isn't much undergrowth—and there are all those dead trees."

Albert thought this over for a moment before ordering the knights to investigate a nearby afflicted tree. The knights who went over soon shouted in surprise.

"What is it?" Albert called.

"Take a look at this. These trees were probably killed by slimes."

Albert and I looked where the knight pointed. An unnatural hole in the trunk began at the ground near the tree's base. It didn't break through to the other side, and it went quite deep. On top of that, the hole seemed to angle beneath the trunk. While the outside of the tree remained, the inside of it might well have been almost hollow.

Around the entrance to the hole were the same shiny marks we had seen at the base of that fallen tree a little earlier. Did that mean a slime had eaten this tree? Had the other dead trees been similarly devoured?

"There's leftover residue here, too."

"And here."

Knights piped up with similar observations about other nearby trees. All the other dead trees we had seen had probably died due to the same reason. We had only just noticed.

"What should we do, Knight Commander? Keep going?"

Albert touched his chin and sank into thought at the knight's question.

I was getting a really bad feeling from the increasing number of slimes and dead trees, but a part of me also wanted to keep going—to find out for sure just how bad the situation was.

I didn't know if Albert sensed my thoughts, but he glanced my way. I didn't know the meaning behind that look, but I nodded. I wanted to keep going. He seemed to catch my drift. He informed the knights that we would continue, and off we went.

Just as expected, the farther we walked, the more dead trees we found, and the scenery grew barren. Along the way, a slime dropped down from a tree that still had leaves, frightening me half to death. On top of that, it fell right next to me. Although I didn't shriek, I felt an indescribable revulsion and reflexively stamped my feet while rubbing my arms.

I decided to pretend I didn't see Albert giving me an

odd look while I acted like a weirdo. *Come on, dropping down from above like that is a mighty attack!*

"Maybe we should head back soon," Albert said as I got my shuddering under control.

It seemed he was using my reaction as a kind of barometer.

We had planned to stay overnight at a nearby village so we could range into the forest farther than we had before. However, if we didn't turn back soon, we'd be stuck spending the night in a forest full of slimes. Although the knights could stand guard in shifts, it would definitely be more dangerous.

The knights nodded to Albert, having thought the same thing. As we were all in agreement, we headed back in the direction from which we had come.

Not long after, Albert's expression suddenly turned dark.

"What's wrong?" I asked.

"Quiet."

The knights around us stopped as well, and tension hung thick in the air. Was it a monster? I held my breath and listened carefully. Sometimes, I heard the shaking of tree leaves.

"Here they come!" a knight shouted.

"What the?!"

Numerous slimes oozed out of the hollow of a dead tree, making the knights cry out in surprise. The slimes seeped out like tree sap, and they were several times larger than the ones we had seen up until then.

At first everyone zeroed in on the slimes. Then I heard a knight gasp as he surveyed the area. I followed his gaze to find more slimes oozing out of the other dead trees as well. On top of being the biggest slimes we had yet seen, we'd never faced such a great number of them at once. I looked to the mage standing next to me. Her face was pale. Oh, boy. We were in big trouble, then.

"Ice Wall," Albert chanted, and a barrier of ice surged up at his command. He cast the spell over and over until we were surrounded by ice shields in every direction but forward.

"I'm sure they'll devour it before long, but it's better than nothing," Albert said.

"And at least this way we won't have to worry about the rear," another knight added.

In other words, we were still surrounded, but at least we had a bit of protection—for now. Just as Albert finished, the battle began.

Albert and the mage were the only ones attacking the slimes. The knights knocked the oncoming slimes back, making sure they came no closer than we could afford. I focused on healing and removing status effects.

This battle went on for much longer than the others had. The ice barrier was slowly eroded, and soon it looked like holes might open in it. Albert noticed these and cast Ice Wall again between salvos.

He was soon low on MP and had to take an MP potion out of the pouch at his belt. He had to down these much more frequently than the mage did, presumably on account of having less total MP. Even if he was likely at least ten levels higher than her at base level, the maximum magical power of a knight and mage no doubt differed a great deal.

I had prepared potions to accommodate for this, but we would run out of those eventually. Yet, no matter how many slimes they killed, the monsters' ranks showed no sign of thinning. Were more coming from the heart of the forest? I feared the situation was getting worse, and I looked up at the sky.

Huh?

It looked like the branches above were reflecting the sunlight. I strained my eyes to see them better. I thought at first that I imagined it, but I wasn't. Slimes clung to the branches of the trees directly overhead. I could guess what would happen next. My blood ran cold.

"They're coming from above, too!" I cried.

Albert stared up and his eyes went wide.

It was as if my voice had been the signal. The slimes dropped one after another onto Albert.

He was in deadly danger—and the moment I saw that, the magic surged up within me. I threw out a wave of the Saint's golden magic to purge the slimes around us. Because I was in a fearful rush, the area of the spell was comparatively small, but it took out all the slimes overhead and within a fifteen-foot radius.

"Can you do that again, Sei?" Albert called.

"Yes!"

"Think you can pave a way for us to get out of here? In that direction!"

"Yes!"

"All right, we're retreating!"

I was pretty sure I had it in me to cast the spell again. I had to.

At Albert's command, the knights who had gone ahead returned to the rear.

Meanwhile, the slimes massed again, and I cast the spell in a line in the direction Albert was pointing. All the slimes caught within the spell line vanished, and the way cleared.

We ran as fast as we could before the slimes could fill the gap, and somehow, we managed to escape the danger.

◆ ◆ ◆

A week had passed since our return from that frantic expedition.

We were all exhausted after and decided to return to Lord Klausner's castle ahead of schedule. Exhaustion wasn't the only reason why. The slimes were a real problem. Our current team was ineffective against monsters that resisted physical attacks. We needed to request more mages from the palace if we were to move forward into the heart of the forest.

Of course, we also needed to inform Lord Klausner of the slimes. We headed straight to him as soon as we arrived at the castle.

Lord Klausner's expression grew quite grim as he listened to the details of our story. While tricky monsters that required magic to fight concerned him, the destruction of the forest was the bigger issue. Corinna, also present, wore the same expression as Lord Klausner. These slimes that could wreak havoc on plant life posed a serious problem for Klausner's Domain, which thrived on exporting herbs.

Corinna's brows knit, forming a deep wrinkle, especially when I told her I hadn't seen a number of the herbs she had told me would be in the forest.

After we finished our report, Albert set about writing a letter requesting reinforcements that was sent to the capital. According to him, the request would likely be accepted, and he believed more mages would arrive soon enough.

While we waited, we didn't sit around twiddling our thumbs. Instead, we continued slaying monsters everywhere not already overrun by slimes. They weren't the only monsters in the forest, after all.

That was how we spent our days. All too soon, it felt like we had eliminated monsters in every stretch of the forest but for the slime wood, and things started to come to a bit of a lull.

As a result—and perhaps it was because we had been so focused on slaying monsters—Albert ordered me to take some time off. He was serious, too. He even forbade me from setting foot inside the brewery. He was so dead set about this that he told Corinna beforehand, so I had to give up on making potions *and* monitoring my herbs.

Thus, I had a free day. No monster slaying, no brewery, no fields, no nothing. I was bored out of my mind.

That meant I had only one other place I could possibly go. I felt bad for imposing on the castle chefs, but I borrowed a corner of the kitchens to bake cookies.

Wasn't cooking considered working? Nah. It made for a good break for me!

First, I measured the ingredients. As I did, the chefs cooking nearby noticed the rosemary on my counter. They grew curious and peered at my work with keen interest.

The people in Salutania weren't familiar with the practice, but herbs could be used in cookies, too. Not to mention, adding herbs meant I could harness the buffing effects brought on by my Cooking skill.

Why was I thinking about that? Well, I was considering bringing these cookies along on our next expedition. You heard me. I was baking cookies not to make snacks for myself but to have something that would be easy to eat on the field, especially since we couldn't always sit down and eat a big meal in the middle of a particularly fraught expedition. So, I wanted to try making something we could snack on instead.

Then I remembered nutrition bars. I had downed those all the time back in Japan. The ones I had in mind were made out of a cookie base similar to shortbread. That thought led to me coming up with something that would be easy to bring along—hence, walnut and rosemary cookies.

"Are you making confections today?" the head chef

asked as I sifted flour. She seemed especially interested in my project.

"Yes, but not exactly—something that will make you feel full."

"Is that so? Is that why you aren't using much sugar?"

"I do want them to be only a little sweet, but mostly it's because sugar is so expensive."

"Ah, that makes sense." She smiled with understanding.

In this world, sweet foods were terribly pricey. Honestly, I wished I could use sugar without so much reserve.

As I chatted with the head chef, I kneaded the dough, shaped the cookies, and baked them in the oven. Finally, they were done. They had a nice golden-brown color to them. I waited for them to cool a bit before picking one up.

All right, these seem pretty good. The slight hint of rosemary gave them a tempting aroma, and the walnuts had a pleasing texture. I wished they were a bit sweeter, but since we would be eating them during an expedition, they were probably best as they were. But if I *did* want them sweeter, maybe I could try adding dried fruit? Although that would cost extra, too... I mulled all this over while I chewed on one.

Then I felt a gaze on my back. I turned to find not only the head chef but all the other chefs looking at me.

"Do you want to try them, too?" I asked tentatively.

They all nodded vigorously. I couldn't help but smile bashfully. The chefs were as enthusiastic as the members of the brewery when it came to learning something new.

Since this was just a test batch, I hadn't made that many cookies, so I apologized for only having enough for one cookie per person. But when I told them that I wanted to make the cookies slighter sweeter, they all gave me lots of different ideas, so it definitely worked out in the end.

Later, I brought some of the cookies to Albert's office, as I thought it would be a good idea to let him try them as well, given that he was in charge of our expeditions.

When I entered and said I had brought him refreshments, he gave me the most dazzling smile. For some reason, I felt like he had increased his attack power since the palace, but maybe it was just my imagination.

He was just about to take a break, so he invited me for tea, just like he had done before. I happily accepted, since I wanted to hear his opinion.

"How are they?" I asked.

"They're wonderful. We could easily bring these along as rations, no question."

"Excellent."

I was glad that he liked them so much. The flavor was rather mild, but they seemed to be just the right level of sweetness for someone like Albert, who wasn't a fan of sweets to begin with. Additionally, he gave me his seal of approval for my expedition supplement plan—perfect.

"I thought I told you to take today off," Albert said as he held up his second cookie.

"I know. That's why I baked these—for stress relief."

He smiled humorlessly. "I see."

And here I'd thought that would be a good answer! But as I had made these as a test batch for the expeditions, from Albert's point of view, it probably did look like I had been working.

Johan often told me that days off were for relaxing, but I was relaxing plenty if you asked me. I hadn't done any real work. My jobs were researching herbs and giving support during expeditions. But maybe this did count? ...Did it?

As Albert and I sipped our tea, rushed footsteps pounded down the hallway. Albert and I exchanged inquisitive looks just as someone knocked frantically at the door. Albert invited them in; it was his retainer, surprisingly out of breath.

"What is it?" Albert asked.

"A messenger from Lord Klausner, sir. The reinforcement mages have arrived from the palace."

"Really?" Albert said dubiously. He had good reason to be surprised. We had sent a request, yes, but it was far too soon for the reinforcements to have actually reached us. We had expected they wouldn't be here for at least another week.

What was going on?

The retainer agreed. Lord Klausner had apparently felt the same and had sent for Albert to help handle this situation. Nothing was going to be solved over teatime, so we decided to go see what exactly these "mages" were up to.

One of the castle servants led us to the square that had become our rendezvous point for expeditions. There, we found a crowd of both knights and palace mages—all freshly arrived from the palace.

I spotted a familiar face among the sea of unfamiliar people and couldn't help but cry out. "Aira?!"

"Sei!"

I couldn't believe it. In front of me stood Aira, clad in the cloak of the Royal Magi Assembly.

"Huh? What are you doing here?" I asked.

"Uh, well, stuff happened, and, ah..." Aira wore an anxious expression that looked almost like a half-smile.

I had known Aira was planning to join the Royal Magi Assembly after she graduated from the Royal Academy, so it wasn't *that* strange to see her as a member of the reinforcements. However, it was still way too soon for the reinforcements to be here. Also, the ratio of knights-to-mages was the strangest thing of all.

The letter to the palace had explicitly requested they dispatch every mage they could to deal with the slimes. Yet this new group had only brought as many mages as our original party had brought when we set out.

Okay, Aira, exactly what kind of "stuff" happened, hm?

Just as I was about to ask, I noticed someone approaching me at a fast pace. They were cloaked in the Royal Magi Assembly robes and had their hood up, covering their face. Aira's smile grew even stiffer.

Albert stepped between the person and me. However, this mage walked up to us with complete disregard for our wariness and threw bzack his hood. Albert and I cried out in surprise.

"It's so nice to see you again!"

There before us was the beautiful smile of Grand Magus Yuri Drewes on his incomparably lovely face—a face we had both assumed would still be at the palace. The way he smiled with his head tilted to the side made me feel like he was actually saying "What do you know, here I am!"

The Saint's*
*Magic Power is *
Omnipotent

Behind the Scenes

"**W**HAT IS THE MEANING of this?!"

Grand Magus Yuri stormed through the main work room in the Royal Magi Assembly's headquarters, which was currently occupied by most of the assembly's mages. The way Yuri barged in without knocking and strode through the hall made the other mages stare up at him in surprise.

However, Magus Erhart didn't look up from the document in his hand even as Yuri slammed his hands on Erhart's desk. Instead, he asked with an unconcerned expression, "What's the meaning of what?"

Tension filled the room, and the other mages paled.

"You know exactly what! Why have they already departed?!" Yuri demanded.

Erhart looked up at him, utterly cool. He had predicted this temper tantrum.

After the king decided to send Sei to the countryside, the most complicated part of the endeavor had been sorting out who would accompany her. It went without saying that either the Knights of the Second Order, who worshipped Sei, or the Third Order, who Sei got along with best, would escort her. From the start, Yuri had insisted he should go, too, and he had refused to bend on the matter.

However, it had already been unusual for both a knight commander *and* the grand magus to participate in an expedition, as had just happened on their mission into Ghoshe Forest. They had concentrated more firepower in that venture than an expedition generally required, and most notably, in so doing they had weakened the palace's own defenses.

They had nevertheless received permission to do it. Firstly, they had been escorting the Saint, whose safety was of paramount importance. Secondly, in their prior expedition into Ghoshe, their troops had suffered terrible injuries. Lastly, the western forest was close to the capital; if anything had happened at the palace, they would have been able to return at once. With these reasons—and careful logistical planning—Yuri had been allowed to go.

However, this time, Sei was headed into the country-side. If some trouble were to befall the capital, neither Sei nor her escorts would be able to return right away. Therefore, it was inconceivable for two leaders of the armed forces—let alone more—to go with her.

Not to mention, despite Yuri's desires, given that he was prone to acting on his own and therefore unfit to lead a whole monster-slaying expedition, he had never been in the running.

All the same, once Sei was set to go, Erhart had predicted that Yuri wouldn't give up or listen to reason—he wanted too fiercely to see Sei in action.

Yuri had missed the exact moment the Saint used her powers in the western forest, since he had been so busy dealing with monsters. Although, when Sei had left the capital, she still hadn't been able to use her Saintly powers at will, there was a high possibility that another black swamp awaited the expedition somewhere in Klausner's Domain. That meant a high possibility that Sei would use the Saint's magic again.

Yuri would never knowingly let this chance slip by. So, Erhart devised a plan. It had been hard to pull off, but in short, he'd moved the date of Sei's departure without alerting Yuri.

To be exact, he'd just told Yuri the wrong date—

specifically a later one. However, expeditions required preparations, and Yuri had been bound to suspect something was up if he noticed this. Therefore, Erhart had asked his little brother Albert to help him disguise those preparations. Albert's position as knight commander of the Third Order had enabled him to do so. In return, Erhart nominated the Third Order to escort Sei. It went without saying that Albert had happily agreed to these terms.

Albert wasn't the only one Erhart had recruited in order to pull off this deception. He had also entreated Johan for help, not only because he was the head of the research institute but because Sei worked for him.

The research institute regularly made potions for the Orders, so they were deeply involved with all preparations for expeditions. Also, Sei frequently met with Yuri since she took magic lessons from him. There was a high chance Sei might let the real date of her departure slip, so it had been necessary to ask Johan to either instruct Sei to keep quiet about the actual date or to give Sei a fake departure date.

Thankfully, both Sei and Johan knew Yuri's personality quite well, so they'd quickly come to an accord. Johan in particular had been all too happy to help; he sympathized with Erhart having to deal with Yuri day in and day out. This might have been because—without naming any names—he also had to work hard to clean up the messes a certain overenthusiastic employee often made.

"Apparently, they decided to move up the date of their departure," Erhart said to Yuri.

"Did they now? I heard nothing of this."

"You weren't going at any rate. They didn't need to tell you."

"I'm the leader of the Assembly."

"But you never do any logistical work, now, do you? Why would they have needed to tell you about a schedule?"

Yuri shut up at that.

Yuri had no interest in his rank or position; he was happy so long as he was able to conduct his research. However, the nobles who had adopted him were particular about status, and he had wound up grand magus partially as a result of their strong backing. Consequently, Erhart—second son of the Hawke family, who oversaw the military of the Kingdom of Salutania— had been appointed magus to serve as Yuri's assistant. This had been critical not only because Yuri's commoner background had left him without any military training but because, again, he had no interest in anything other than research.

In any case, it was a well-known fact that Yuri was grand magus in name only. Even Yuri agreed with this and was largely pleased about it. He was happy to be able to devote himself to his work and frequently used it as an excuse to leave all the paperwork to Erhart.

As Erhart regularly had to do both the job of the magus and that of the grand magus, he suffered from a lot more headaches than he should have for one in his position. This time, however, he had used the situation to his advantage, and he had clearly been rewarded for his hard work.

"Paperwork aside, I *do* go out to help slay monsters. Therefore, shouldn't I be told everything related to expeditions?" Yuri asked.

"You're not going to back down, are you? You weren't possibly planning to secretly slip in with them, were you?" Erhart asked, his questions like daggers.

Although Yuri flinched, he pouted right away—proof that Erhart was spot-on.

Erhart sighed with both relief and exasperation. "I'm pretty sure I explained why you can't join this time."

Despite Erhart's accusatory look, Yuri continued to sulk, which only made Erhart sigh again. However, Erhart was grateful he had stopped Yuri's recklessness for once. He proceeded to assign some of the paperwork on his desk to his errant grand magus. "Maybe you'll learn something from doing this once in a while, too."

After that tiff, the Royal Magi Assembly returned to its normal everyday life, at least for a while. But the situation changed after one of Albert's periodic reports arrived at the palace.

"It sounds like there are indeed many more monsters now in Klausner's Domain," the king said.

"Yes. However, at present, they're managing the situation without any difficulties," the prime minister replied.

"They haven't found the swamp yet?"

"I'm afraid not. But Knight Commander Hawke confirms that he believes there might well be one."

The day after the report arrived, the prime minister summoned Erhart along with the leaders of the other martial orders. They gathered in a designated room to hear the prime minister's briefing about the current state of affairs in Klausner's Domain.

The fact that Erhart was summoned despite Yuri being available meant that the prime minister felt this information should be heard by Erhart specifically. Erhart realized why when the prime minister spoke.

"As for the Saint, Knight Commander Hawke reports that she has discovered how to use her powers at will."

"That's heartening news," said the king.

Everyone breathed a sigh of relief—and everyone simultaneously understood exactly why Yuri had not also been called for the meeting.

While Yuri usually projected mild-mannered friendliness in public, he was famous for descending into reckless abandon the second something caught his interest. So strong was his enthusiasm for studying magic that he was widely considered obsessed. He even went monster hunting on his own for the sake of his research—an otherwise unheard of practice. And at present, Yuri's greatest interest was in the Saint's unique magic. Now that Sei could use her powers at will, it was only natural for everyone to fear that he might run off to Klausner's Domain on his own.

The prime minister finished his briefing and looked over the gathered. "Are there any questions?"

Knight Commander Rudolf Aiblinger of the Knights of the Second Order raised his hand. All eyes focused on him. "You said they have yet to find the black swamp. Will they not need more help to aid their search?"

"I don't believe so. They're working with the local mercenary company to search the entire domain. It's only a matter of time before they locate it," the prime minister said with a hint of exasperation. He sensed Rudolf's true intentions.

Many members in the Second Order worshiped Sei. Her first public use of Holy Magic had been to heal a hospital full of injured knights. These knights had just returned from an ill-fated expedition into Ghoshe Forest during which the Second and Third Orders had worked together. As such, numerous knights from the Second Order had been among those she healed.

The spell Sei used at that moment had been so powerful that multiple knights had regrown arms and legs they had lost in battle—an astounding triumph of magical power. Many of the knights who worshiped Sei now were the ones who had on that day recovered missing parts of their bodies.

First on the list of worshippers was Rudolf's second-in-command. It was now well-known that, when the man learned the Third Order had been selected to escort the Saint, he had fallen to his knees in despair, heedless of who might be watching.

To wit, Rudolf was trying to fix a morale problem. His second-in-command and some of his knights had taken to cursing his name when he wasn't around, and he hoped this would be an opportunity to send some of his men to the Saint's side, thereby alleviating some of their frustration. No one wanted their subordinates cursing them.

The prime minister knew very well what Rudolf was angling for, and he understood the situation.

"But don't we need to find the swamp as soon as possible though?" Rudolf asked.

"There are fewer monsters in Klausner's Domain now, thanks to the Saint's arrival. There's no need to rush in with more manpower than they already have," the prime minister said.

"But I understand there will be far more fiends in the vicinity of a black swamp. Should we not send more men ahead of time?"

"The Third Order has experience dealing with a swamp from their prior expedition in Ghoshe Forest. It is of course dangerous, but I'm sure they will put their previous experience to use and deal with it efficiently enough at their current numbers."

Rudolf frowned at this prompt rejection.

However, the prime minister didn't want to send any more troops than necessary to Klausner's Domain. Dispatching more people meant reallocating supplies and various other costly necessities.

Ultimately, the meeting came to an end with a decision to continue monitoring the situation.

Several days after that meeting, Erhart got a bad feeling. He hadn't seen Yuri since that morning. Normally, he just assumed Yuri was slacking off on the practice grounds, but he had a sneaking feeling that this wasn't the case.

He asked one of the mages to run to the practice grounds and look for Yuri while he himself set off for the grand work hall where the rest of the mages usually gathered. When he reached it, he scanned the crowd and confirmed that Yuri was not in evidence. When he started questioning the mages, he got a surprising response.

"So, he went monster hunting?" Erhart asked.

"Y-yes, that's right."

"By himself?"

"No, he took some others with him."

At this, Erhart frowned. Yuri headed into the nearby forest in order to hone his magical prowess relatively often. However, he rarely—if ever—brought anyone along with him.

When Erhart asked who exactly Yuri had brought, the answer made his frown deepen. One of the people Yuri had taken was Aira.

While Yuri denied this, some secretly thought that Aira, who had been summoned together with Sei, might be another Saint. These same people thought Aira had been accepted into the Royal Magi Assembly specifically to nurture her Saintly abilities. Whatever the reason, Aira received somewhat unusual treatment from time to time.

This being the case, anyone who thought Yuri was acting strangely brushed it off once he took Aira with him. They figured whatever he was up to had to do with her, so they hadn't tried to stop him.

Erhart dragged his hand down his face.

At that moment, Knight Commander Rudolf of the Second Order rushed into the room, looking panicked. All the mages' eyes turned to him. Rudolf took a moment to catch his breath, a grim expression on his face. He then strode over to Erhart.

Erhart frowned at Rudolf; his bad feeling had only intensified. "Has something happened?"

"Some of my knights have gone on an expedition with some mages."

"An expedition, you say?"

"Yes. Apparently, they told everyone that they intended to pursue a giant monster in the western forest. But I have reports to suggest this is false."

"Then where did they go?"

"In the direction of Klausner's Domain."

A vein in Erhart's temple throbbed. The mages standing close to him quietly backed away.

In Erhart's opinion, this was all Yuri's doing, but Rudolf had another hypothesis. All the knights who had disappeared were the ones who had most fervently yearned to escort Sei to Klausner's Domain. Rudolf suspected that his knights had planned this and brought Erhart's mages along to make it look like they were going on a routine expedition.

Once they were found out, the people who had planned this would doubtless be punished. If they had gone forward with it anyway, they truly did care more about Sei than any retaliation. Their adoration of her was indeed something to be feared.

Notably, Rudolf's second-in-command had been left behind. It was possible the knights had feared this infraction would become more serious if they included him.

"I'm very sorry your people got dragged into this," Rudolf said.

Erhart sighed. "No, it was probably our people doing the dragging."

"What do you mean?"

"The whereabouts of the grand magus are currently unknown."

For a moment, Rudolf gaped at Erhart, but he swiftly recovered himself and suggested they both seek out the prime minister. Things being as they were, Rudolf recommended they do so with all speed. Erhart weakly nodded.

In the end, the two of them left the Assembly's headquarters at very near a run.

A bit earlier, Aira had found herself standing in the square that served as the rendezvous point for troops before they departed on expeditions. She watched as knights from the Second Order busily piled supplies in wagons.

Normally, Aira would have spent the day doing clerical work in the Royal Magi Assembly's barracks. Yet here she was in this square on Grand Magus Yuri's orders. She had been doing her work as usual when he'd casually announced to the hall that he was going on an expedition and then swept her up along with him.

Aira wasn't the only one who'd been whisked off in that moment. Honestly, it felt a bit like Yuri had randomly recruited the mages nearest to him when he made his declaration, and Aira had just happened to be included.

In truth, Aira was right to think that. Yuri hadn't been thinking about anything like "team fit" when he selected his handful of mages.

Aira felt uneasy as she stood in the midst of everyone making their preparations to go. It wasn't the expedition itself she worried about. She usually looked forward to them, in fact. After her graduation from the Royal Academy, she'd joined the Royal Magi Assembly, and she had gone on several expeditions as part of her new job. She was quite used to them now, especially compared to the very first time she had faced a monster. She still got nervous, but monster hunting just didn't make her anxious anymore.

Plus, they were heading into the western forest, known as Ghoshe Forest. Ghoshe had once been famous for being rife with monsters, but ever since Sei had gone into it, hardly any had appeared there. And if there were new monsters, there was no way they'd be nearly as numerous as they had been when Sei and the Third Order went to face them.

However, since a large monster had been spotted on the edge of the forest, everyone was in a hurry to slay it, and the grand magus was with them. He had zero interest in anything but magic, and partially because of that, he was terribly powerful. No matter if it was one big monster or many, Aira couldn't imagine they would be in danger if Yuri was going to be with them—especially not since he was so well known for loving the heat of battle.

Then why did she feel so uneasy? Aira really wasn't sure. But as she stood there watching everyone, she felt, somehow, like they were bringing more supplies than they needed.

A little while later, everything was packed, and they departed. It would take some time to get to the western forest, so most people rode in covered wagons as they went. All the mages were piled into one of the wagons together.

The wagon had a canopy, and benches lined both sides. Seats weren't assigned, so they all just sat in the order they came into the wagon. Aira's seat happened to be right in the middle of one of the benches.

Along the way, Aira discussed the monster they thought they were going after with her peers. When they were done talking strategy, they shifted to just chatting.

Suddenly curious, Aira looked in Yuri's direction. He was seated directly across from her, and he hadn't really said much the whole time. He looked lost in thought.

I wonder what he's thinking about?

The first time Aira had met him, she had been astonished by his good looks—a face so perfectly lovely that it almost seemed fake. She hadn't been able to take her eyes off of him. Now she was quite used to being around him since they worked together. If she had only ever seen

Yuri from afar, she probably would have continued to be entirely charmed, but seeing his exchanges with Erhart every day had fixed that.

In other words, the exquisite illusion had swiftly been destroyed. At least he was still nice to look at.

Basically, Aira wasn't peering at him because she was captivated by his face. However, while she was studying him, their eyes met.

"What?" Yuri asked.

"Uh, nothing..." Aira trailed off.

Now it was Yuri's turn to study her closely as she shifted her gaze away. She managed to ignore him for a time, but she soon became all too aware that he was still looking at her. Unable to endure it any longer, she slowly returned her gaze to him.

Although they were both part of the Royal Magi Assembly, Yuri was the grand magus and Aira was just a regular mage—they barely came into actual contact with one another. Also, although Aira had been summoned with Sei during the Saint Summoning Ritual, because she couldn't use the Saint's powers, Yuri had zero interest in her. They had never even talked. Moreover, Aira wasn't the type to talk to her superiors without a good reason to, so she hadn't really tried to change that. As a result, Aira was hesitant to ask Yuri idle questions, but she couldn't come up with a good answer, so she wound up just being honest.

"You looked like you were lost in thought about something, so I was wondering what it was."

"Ah. I was thinking about magic."

Aira and Yuri's voices were the only sounds in the wagon. Everyone else had gone silent. The other mages had all stopped chatting to listen to what interesting new thing this rare exchange might provide.

However, Yuri's answer was pretty typical for him. Aira could see why everyone said he was fixated.

"What about magic?" she asked, nevertheless.

"The Saint's, in particular."

"You mean Sei's?" Aira asked.

Yuri's eyes widened slightly in surprise to hear Aira address Sei by name. "You know her? That must mean..." Yuri stopped as something seemed to occur to him. He peered closely at her face.

Aira had known a number of attractive people back at the Academy, but to have someone so pretty—who was also her boss—stare at her like that made her a bit uncomfortable. But that unpleasantness didn't last long.

A moment later, Yuri touched his chin and nodded, having come to a conclusion: "You're the girl who came from her world."

Hadn't he known that? "Th-that's right."

"Hmm, I see." He sank into thought again.

Aira tilted her head, confused, but then Yuri asked her another question. "Do you talk to Sei often?"

"Huh? No? Maybe? Maybe more than some other people. We have tea once in a while."

"I see. That sounds like often to me."

From an objective point of view, Aira wasn't sure she had that many opportunities to converse with Sei. Realistically, compared to Sei's coworkers at the Research Institute of Medicinal Flora, she didn't get to see Sei all that much. However, if you took everyone in the palace into consideration, she was probably more in the "often" group.

At any rate, besides the institute, Sei only ever went to the Order and Assembly barracks and the palace library. Her circle of friends was naturally quite small. The fact that Aira was close enough to have tea with Sei meant she was actually *rather* close to her. At the very least, Sei didn't have any other friends in the Royal Magi Assembly aside from Yuri and Erhart.

Although to be clear, Yuri concluded Aira and Sei were close mostly because they had come from the same world.

"What do you two talk about when you're together?" he asked.

"Oh, hm. I guess we talk about things happening in our day to day lives. And about Japan, the country we came from."

"If you talk about your daily lives, does that mean you talk about magic, too?"

"A bit. We run into one another at the practice grounds sometimes, so it's mostly there."

"Has she ever talked to you about the Saint's magic?"

"A little. She was rather frustrated that she couldn't figure out how to get it to work."

"So she still doesn't know. I wondered."

Other people would probably have been more interested to hear more about the other world they'd come from, but Yuri remained true to his nature.

Yuri had realized Sei was trying to hide her Sainthood from the moment he tried to Appraise her stats. At that point, he had considered it possible that Sei was claiming she couldn't use her Saintly powers at will even though she actually could. However, from his interactions with Sei, he had decided it was likely she was telling the truth. He asked Aira anyway just to make sure. He figured that if Aira was a friend from the same world, Sei might have divulged information to her that she would have kept from him.

Aira realized what Yuri was angling for when he bullishly steered the conversation toward the topic. She was aware that Sei didn't really like how she had been thrust into the vaunted position of Saint, so Aira tried to put what she knew in a way so it wouldn't upset her friend. After all, Yuri already knew a lot about what Aira mentioned.

In short, Sei couldn't use her powers at will—no inconsistencies there.

(Notably, Aira didn't mention that Sei often complained about Yuri's grueling special training.)

There was nothing new for Yuri to learn from this conversation, but since they were already on his favorite subject, he easily came up with new topics to entertain himself. He was especially interested in channeling.

Aira mentioned that Sei had talked about the usefulness of magical manipulation when making potions, and Yuri nodded, saying she was probably onto something. Meanwhile, the other mages murmured to each other. This was the first time they were hearing of such things.

Soon, they were all congenially bantering away, so it took a while for anyone to speak up about a certain other matter. One mage sitting near the back of the wagon was the first to do so, and he looked somewhat perturbed as he said, "Hey, aren't we going the wrong way?"

"What do you mean?"

"Huh?"

The other mages sitting near the opening looked out of the canopy, and as they did, their expressions changed. They had all been to the western forest several times before, but outside the canopy, they saw an unfamiliar landscape. However, the coachman of the wagon behind them didn't seem the least bit concerned.

The wagon filled with voices wondering what was going on. Their panic revived the unease Aira had felt when they departed. Her expression darkened as she realized that bad feeling had been accurate all along.

You're supposed to look to your boss in times like these, right? Aira thought as she turned to Yuri.

Hand on his chin, Yuri wore the hint of a smile on his lips. How odd.

"Grand Magus?" Aira asked suspiciously.

The other mages turned to Yuri as well. The clamor quieted as they took in Yuri's serenity.

"Do you know where we are now?" Yuri quietly asked.

"I cannot say for certain, but we appear to be heading much farther west than Ghoshe Forest," the mage by the back said, making Yuri smile all the more.

The mages all exchanged a look.

"Do you know where we're headed, Grand Magus?" one asked.

"No, I don't. But I think I can guess."

"Where, then?"

"Klausner's Domain, most likely."

The mages looked shaken. Several of them clearly remembered Yuri saying they were going to go take on a monster in Ghoshe Forest—and they could confirm this with each other. Yet it didn't seem like Yuri had lied to them either.

"The request was to accompany the Second Order to the western forest, right?" one of the mages asked.

"That's right," said Yuri.

"Then why would you think we're heading somewhere else?"

"Because of how many supplies they packed into the wagons. And also, the fact that this request came from the *Second* Order."

I knew it, Aira thought.

"Supplies aside, what does the Second Order have to do with it?" one mage asked.

Yuri chuckled. "Well, you see, there are just so many knights in the Second Order who simply adore the Lady Saint. And they must have been grief-stricken that they weren't selected to escort her to Klausner's Domain."

The mages exchanged another look. Their faces paled as they grasped the gravity of their situation.

"I decided to join this expedition on a whim, and I'm so glad I did." Yuri smiled brightly.

Now the mages were just perplexed—how were they going to deal with this?

Although they couldn't confirm exactly where they were going, Yuri's mood suggested they definitely weren't headed back to the capital any time soon, at least. They couldn't imagine he would agree to turn around. He wanted to go to Klausner's Domain as much as these Second Order knights. And though he claimed he hadn't known where the knights were going, the mages couldn't rule out the idea that he might have been in cahoots with the knights from the beginning.

At any rate, they were presently stuck going to Klausner's Domain whether they liked it or not. No matter how they might protest, the only person who could actually stop Yuri—Erhart—wasn't there.

At least, even if they did get in trouble later, their carefree boss was sure to take the brunt of the punishment. And even if they didn't send up some sort of emergency signal, their brilliant magus was sure to figure out what had happened sooner or later.

The mages all realized this as they looked helplessly at each other and sighed simultaneously, giving up on the idea of reining Yuri in—let alone the rest of this new expedition.

The Saint's
Magic Power is
Omnipotent

ACT
3
Experiments

ALL RIGHT! These little guys are looking really good." I couldn't help but smile as I looked at the herbs in the pots I had blessed. Their leaves glistened in the rays of the morning sun.

They were growing well. Maybe too well. Actually, I had a feeling they were growing faster than normal. I also had a feeling that Corinna, who was monitoring their development with me, had noticed as much.

It would soon be time to move to the next stage of my experiment: blessing a small field. We would head back to the capital as soon as we fixed the monster problem in Klausner's Domain, so it wasn't like I had forever. Optimally, I would fix both problems quickly.

Meanwhile, since reinforcements from the capital had arrived without warning, Albert was busy working out the new squad formations. Although Grand Magus Yuri had come along with the reinforcements, he wasn't exactly backup for Albert, so to speak. He often went monster hunting on his own, so he was no help figuring out a team-based strategy. More accurately, he had no experience with teamwork.

I had my doubts about whether someone like that should hold a leadership position, but the whole matter was complicated. Probably.

Other mages had come with Yuri as well, although not in nearly the numbers we had requested. Therefore, Albert had to assign a mostly mage squad to tackle the slime wood while the remaining mages would be scattered among the squads taking care of other regions.

Albert had a lot of experience organizing teams, so ordinarily this wouldn't have taken him too long. But the knights from the Second Order had complicated things. All of them wanted to go to the slime wood, so things were getting messy. I learned about this from a Third Order knight who liked to gossip with me. According to him, things certainly didn't sound good.

In any case, we were sure to head out again once Albert got the squads figured out, so I wanted to make as much progress as I could with my experiments now. No time to waste, as they say.

Once I checked the plants, I headed straight over to the brewery. There, I updated Corinna on their condition and told her what I wanted to try next. Corinna had also kept a daily eye on the pots, so she knew it was time for the next stage as well. She immediately accepted my request to try blessing a field. In fact, she already had a field ready for me to bless and said that we could head over there right away.

Corinna seemed over the moon to be able to start growing plants she had lost the ability to cultivate. She had that skip in her step all the way out to the field.

"Wait, it's okay if I use this whole thing?" I asked when we got there.

"Yes. We already have Lord Klausner's permission."

She had brought me to a wide, tilled field. I could see the forest way off in the distance, but this field truly was vast. I supposed you needed this much space to properly experiment with a variety of herbs.

But was it really all right for me to use so much space? I hesitated, but Corinna urged me on, so I pulled myself together and called up my magic.

It was embarrassing to cast the Saint's magic in front of others, but I set those feelings aside for now. And anyway, Corinna had seen me bless the original experimental pots. Better not to think too deeply about it either way.

I inhaled and concentrated on the magic. After a few moments, I sensed my power floating lightly in the air. Not good enough. I continued concentrating, pushing the scope of the magic farther and farther. I stopped it only when the magic had spread to cover a healthy fraction of the field and released the held power, all while wishing for the herbs to grow.

"Was that the Saint's magic just now?" I heard someone ask just as the earth of the field glowed white.

I turned with a jolt to find Yuri walking toward me from the direction of the city with that ever-lovely smile across his face. Corinna looked surprised as well. She hadn't expected him either. After all, this whole blessing business was classified information for Klausner's Domain. Corinna had even given strict orders telling no one to come by our field for the next few hours. It appeared that Yuri had missed the memo.

While we hadn't exactly been able to loop him in on the instructions to stay away, since he wasn't part of Klausner's chain of command, we were potentially in a bit of trouble.

"Good morning," I said as brightly as I could.

"And a good morning to you as well. So, what was that just now?"

"Well, you're right," I said reluctantly. "It was the power of the Saint."

"I knew it! So you *can* use it at will now!"

So much for coming up with a diversion. His face glowed even more than it had before.

Then I frowned. *Wait, did he not know I'd finally made a breakthrough?*

Yuri interrupted my thoughts with yet another question I didn't want to answer. "By the way, why are you using it in a place like this?"

Uhhh, what do I say here? Telling him the truth was off the table, since that would mean exposing Lord Klausner's deception to the palace. "I asked Lord Klausner for a place to practice casting, and he suggested out here."

"Is that so?"

"This field is enormous—and there's nothing growing here. And we figured, you know, the Saint's magic won't do anything *bad* to a field." A pretty weak excuse, if I did say so myself. But for Lord Klausner's sake—and Corinna's—I had to evade the truth. When I glanced nervously at her, her expression remained unchanged.

"I see," said Yuri. "Perhaps the fields wouldn't suffer for your practice, but you might have already affected the soil."

"Huh?"

"For some reason, I feel an unusual power in the soil now," Yuri murmured as he touched his chin and studied the dirt.

I couldn't feel any difference at all, but Yuri sure seemed to detect something with all his expertise.

Yet Corinna's brow twitched. I had a feeling she didn't know who this guy making all these pronouncements was. She glanced at me, so I nodded.

We're okay. He knows magic, but he doesn't know anything about agriculture—I doubt he'd know I "blessed" anything. Although, he might have an inkling as to what we've been up to.

It wasn't like I could convey the particulars, though. I'd have to explain everything to her later.

To the point, the unusual power Yuri sensed had to be my Saint's magic. Yuri had once told me that all living creatures carried magic within them, but was it normal for a nonliving thing like soil to be magical, too? And while we think of soil as just being dirt, it has all sorts of organisms and stuff in it, so did the blessings affect that stuff as well? Or had I enchanted its mineral components? There seemed to be no end to the possibilities once I started thinking about it, and all of it seemed feasible.

When I brought this up, both Yuri and Corinna listened with keen interest. Actually, they had kind of similar expressions. As we discussed, they began exchanging opinions and seemed to both get something out of the conversation. I thought they got along pretty well. That was good and all, but...

"Shall we head to the next location then?" Yuri asked. As he urged me to do more blessings, he wore a smile that would have left any other woman spellbound. He was beyond delighted to finally get a chance to observe the Saint's magic.

For some reason, Corinna nodded in agreement.

It might have been a mistake to tell him I was practicing.

Oh. Hey. Wait. You mean I have to summon the magic with Yuri watching me? No, uh, it takes too much time, and he's a busy—no, that's not right. I-I need to do my own preparations, mentally speaking, or—no. Tell him i-it's just for training? But, I, like, I, what... Nooooooo!

With the occasional break between casts, I used my Saint's magic to systematically bless the whole field. The plan had been for me to perform the blessings and then let the gardeners at it to plant the seeds. So with that done, I left Corinna to direct the gardeners and went with Yuri to the knights' quarters.

I had actually wanted to watch the planting, but Yuri wanted to discuss something, so I had to go with him. In all likelihood, he wanted to talk about my Saintly powers. He had asked me a ton of questions even during my breaks.

When we got to the knights' quarters, Yuri swept through the hall and up to the second floor. I followed behind him, past the knight commander's office, to a room that appeared to be for his personal use. That had to be a perk of being (somehow) the grand magus of the Royal Magi Assembly.

The furniture arrangement was pretty much the same as in Albert's office. The only difference? The number of documents on the desk. Naturally, Albert always had a ton of management-related paperwork. Meanwhile, I was pretty sure the ones scattered on Yuri's desk exclusively related to his own research.

As I looked around the room, Yuri encouraged me to take a seat on one of the sofas. A moment later, a retainer brought over some kind of herbal tea and cookies.

Is this chamomile? It has such a nice fragrance. I gazed at the light amber color in the cup, and just as I took a sip, Yuri started in on pursuing his real interest.

"The Saint's magic uses even more magic power than I had predicted."

"It does," I agreed. In fact, it ate up quite a lot.

Area-of-effect magic usually cost more MP, the cost increasing with potency and range. The Saint's magic was also area-of-effect magic and was likewise affected by scale.

That said, it wasn't like I had been blessing truly big fractions of the field at any given time. Nevertheless, after two rounds, I'd been left nearly drained of MP. That meant blessings required a whole heck of a lot to begin with. Although, I couldn't discount the possibility that blessings used a lot of MP due to their potency more than their range.

Basically, for every two parts of the fields I'd blessed, I had to take a break to recover MP. Yuri had been impatient, but what was I supposed to do? I could have drunk MP potions and kept going, but I didn't want to waste potions during an herb shortage. Besides, MP recovered over time just like HP. You just had to wait a minute.

We weren't in a rush either, so waiting had been no problem. Both Yuri and Corinna understood the consequences of wasting potions, so Yuri had accepted the necessity of a wait...to an extent.

Yuri, being who he was, had asked me questions nonstop while I was resting. He wanted to know everything I had discovered while we'd been apart.

"The next time we go on an expedition, we'll need to ready a number of MP potions, I suspect. Especially now that we have more mages," Yuri said over tea.

"That's true. I think we should probably prepare as many high-grade ones as possible, even with the shortage."

"And perhaps you should train more so you can cast the Saint's magic a bit faster. From what I've seen, you should be able to do speed it up a bit, yes?"

I sank into silence and looked away from Yuri, who had a hand on his chin.

Cast it faster? That would be a bit hard! Or maybe I should say that'd be really *hard.* I had to do so much mental preparation before I cast. But he was probably right that it would be best if I trained a bit more. I could use the magic now, but my timing was actually all over the place. If training could help me be more consistent, then it was a no-brainer.

Before I was even sure of my conclusion, Yuri launched his next attack. "By the way, what *did* wind up being the key to casting the magic at will?"

"Huh?" I turned to him in spite of myself. He repeated the question.

Th-the key, he asks? He's asking me to tell him what I have to do? As in, the thing that makes the magic work? Like, what I have to think about? There's no way I can tell him that!

"Uh..." I said.

I was painfully aware of Yuri's intent and silent gaze as I fretted, my eyes darting back and forth. *It wasn't like there was a specific entry in the Great Alchemist's diary—not that I could even share that with him. I wish she had written a little more about it. Then I could at least say something else!*

"Is it something you find difficult to say?" Yuri pressed.

"Um..." I clammed up.

Yuri nodded. "I see. So it is."

"Uhh..." I knew my behavior was only confirming his suspicions, but the embarrassment made me avert my gaze from him again.

"Well, that's all right. Let's call it here for now."

"Huh?" I looked at Yuri in surprise. Since when had he so easily dropped the subject? He only smiled at me. "Are you sure?" I asked.

"Are you going to tell me?"

"No..."

"No need to feel bad about it. You needn't force yourself to answer. I really don't mind." The extremely beautiful grin he shot my way sent a chill down my spine.

What's he thinking?!

As I shuddered, someone knocked on the door. Yuri invited them in—and just my luck, it was Albert. My heart tried to leap straight up out of my chest.

"Come in, come in," said Yuri.

"Sorry to bother you in the middle of your research," Albert said as he entered. He looked surprised to find me there. From the cookies and the herbal tea on the table, one might have thought we were taking a break, but Albert knew better than to assume Yuri would ever be doing anything but feeding his curiosity.

"I don't mind at all. What can I do for you?" Yuri asked.

"Oh, if you two have something to discuss, I'll excuse myself," I said, and I half-rose to my feet before Albert stopped me.

"No, you should hear this as well," he said. "I finished drawing up the new squads, so I was hoping to get another pair of eyes on the plan."

Is that really what he wants to discuss with me? I gave him a puzzled look as Yuri encouraged him to sit down.

He did. Right next to me.

"Here are the new formations." Albert handed over the sheet with the lists.

Yuri scanned it and nodded. "I take no issues with it."

"Thanks. Then we're set."

"Shouldn't Lady Sei take a look as well?"

"Huh?" *Why me, though?* "Is that okay?"

"I don't mind. Take a look, Sei."

At Albert's permission, Yuri handed the paper to

me. As I looked it over, I realized why Yuri thought it warranted my attention: knights from the Second Order were among those going into the slime wood with me.

Ah, those *guys...* I found a number of names I recognized. These were the knights who always insisted on carrying my books from the palace library to the research institute. Oops, I was getting distracted.

As slimes were so resistant to physical attacks, I had a lot more mages on my team this time around. To be more precise, I had every single mage who could use offensive magic. A few more knights were with us, too, adding up to a much larger group. Albert explained that more mages always meant more knights to protect them. Naturally, the chosen knights had all established reputations for their defensive skills.

Not all of the Second Order would go to the slime wood. The rest would be heading to other parts of the forest at the same time, and since we had more people now, we could run multiple expeditions concurrently.

The other squads also differed from the norm. They either had one mage who could use Healing Magic or they had no mages at all. The squads without magical support would have to power through on potions alone.

I should probably up their potion quota then, I thought.

"So there are a lot of slimes in this forest? I can't wait to take them out," Yuri said.

When I looked up from the paper, Yuri had the most ecstatic look on his face. I knew what that look meant. Those slimes were in critical danger. He had held himself back in Ghoshe Forest, but this time all bets were off.

Please, oh please, don't burn down the slime wood! I begged. That look was *dangerous*.

After that, I returned to the brewery. Now that the new squads were assigned, we would probably head back into the slime wood in a few days.

I got myself pumped up to get potions and stuff all prepped, but Corinna caught me before I could get started. In fact, the second I entered the brewery, Corinna beckoned me over. I followed her into the back room. There, she closed the door. It seemed that whatever she wanted to talk about, she didn't want others to overhear. That probably meant it was about the blessings and Yuri. She had seemed rather concerned about him back at the fields, after all.

"What's the matter?" I asked.

"That person we saw. It sounded like he came from the capital, but just who is he?"

"You mean that man with the navy-blue hair?"

"Yeah, him. The pretty boy. You guys seemed to know one another."

"Yes, he is Lord Drewes, the grand magus of the Royal Magi Assembly."

"The Royal Magi Assembly? It's no wonder then." She nodded in understanding.

Just as I suspected, Yuri's observations had piqued Corinna's interest. When he had pointed out the magic in the soil, she had worried my blessings would be found out, but talking with him after, she realized he hadn't quite caught on.

"You didn't tell him anything, right?" Corinna asked.

"No, no. I understand this is a confidential matter."

"Thank you. I was only asking to make sure."

"Of course. It's part of your job."

"Sorry. For a moment there, I actually thought you might have told him. He was quite the character." Corinna chuckled dryly.

Yuri had gotten really into their conversation and dug into some rather technical arcane concepts. To me, Corinna had seemed to enjoy the conversation, too, but apparently he'd gone off on a number of complex tangents far outside her realm of expertise. For myself, since I'd found everything they were talking about difficult to grasp, I had tuned out halfway through and focused on casting instead.

"He's one we need to keep an eye on, though. I get the feeling he might figure it out even if we don't tell him," Corinna said.

"I wouldn't be surprised if he did."

We had to assume he would. Yuri had done a ton of research on the Saint in order to perform the Saint Summoning Ritual. He probably knew there had been a Saint in Klausner's Domain. And he had noticed the magic power in the soil after I used the Saint's powers. If he put that together with the fact that Klausner's Domain was uniquely able to cultivate certain herbs that couldn't grow anywhere else, then he would soon suspect that past Saint had something to do with it. Soon enough, he'd link the famous Great Alchemist to that past Saint as well.

I had needed the Great Alchemist's diary in order to figure how all those things connected, but Yuri was smart enough that he'd probably be able to put two and two together on his own. He had incredible deductive powers. Given what a research nerd he was, he probably enjoyed the process as much as the result.

Huh?

"What's wrong?" Corinna asked.

"Uh, nothing, I just got this sneaking feeling."

Why? What was the cause? But no matter how much I thought about it, I couldn't figure it out. *Maybe it'll come to me later. I should focus on preparing for the expeditions.*

We dropped the topic of Yuri and blessings, and I finally set about making potions. I consulted with Corinna about the types of potions to prepare—and how many— as we returned to the adjacent workroom.

Then I checked the brewery ledger that listed the herb stock and discovered they didn't have a number of the herbs I needed to make MP potions. I wasn't sure what to do, so I asked Corinna, and she said she'd scrape some together from other distributors in the domain.

We hadn't yet seen the black swamp, but I agreed with the popular opinion—it likely lay in the slime wood. Given this, we could expect our expeditions would soon come to an end, and therefore, now was not the time to be stingy with potions. If we didn't actually find the swamp in the slime wood, we'd just have to bring in herbs from the neighboring towns.

With all this supply chain stuff on the table, I opted to ask Lord Klausner to take care of the logistics. I also asked the brewery alchemists for help—there was just so much that needed to be made. Corinna gave the alchemists one order after another. The brewery soon buzzed with a flurry of activity.

One person went to alert Lord Klausner while others headed to the storehouse for extra herbs and others pulled out their potion-making apparatuses. I was in charge of readying the equipment so I could start making potions as soon as the ingredients arrived. I thanked the folks who had gone to the storehouse when they returned and got to work.

"There's more where that came from. We ordered more in after you started making all those big batches." The alchemist who brought the herbs immediately turned on their heels to get another load.

We had a ton of potions to make and minimal space to put them, so I needed to use up the herbs already on hand to clear precious counter space. To the point, I couldn't lose focus. I rolled up my sleeves and threw the available herbs into a cauldron.

As I stirred, I heard some lively voices behind me. I glanced back to find the mercenaries helping the alchemists haul herbs to the brewery. Leo was among them. He spotted me and raised a hand in greeting. "Hey there!"

"Hi, Leo. What are you up to?"

"Well, I saw some official-looking people carrying a bunch of boxes. When I wandered over to check it out, I realized it was all herbs. You guys are always saving us with your potions, so we decided to pitch in a bit."

"Thank you very much."

I chatted away with Leo and his men while making potions, and they continued to pile wooden boxes along the walls. I began to fear that if I didn't make these potions faster, before long, the whole room would overflow with ingredients.

As I picked up my pace, Leo spoke again. "I'm still amazed by how many you make, you know. You don't usually go for this many, right?"

"Mm-hmm. But there's more knights now, so the next expedition is going to be a bit of a special case."

"Oh, you mean what with the slimes?"

"You heard about those?"

"'Course I did. I'm the leader of the local mercs, in case you forgot. I heard all about it from Lord Klausner."

"I see." Well, duh, that made sense.

"You goin' slime hunting, too?"

"That's right. After all, I can use...some kind of offensive magic?"

"Why you tiltin' your head like that?"

"It's just that my powers are kinda weird."

"Oh, yeah."

It feels a bit wrong to call the Saint's magic offensive, but it's probably accurate, seeing as it does work on monsters, right?

Leo seemed to get what I meant even with my vague answer. "Any mage is a better bet for taking out slimes," he said, helping me cover.

"Yeah... I guess they really don't feel physical hits at all."

"So the knights are just with you for protection?"

Spot on again, Leo. The knights going to the slime wood would be there to escort the mages. However, I didn't think I was strictly authorized to tell Leo exactly what the squad makeups would be, so I just smiled ambiguously. Leo didn't seem to mind the lack of a straight answer and just crossed his arms, looking thoughtful.

What's on his mind now? I absentmindedly glanced at him, curious.

After a few moments, Leo looked up again and frowned a bit. "You stopped working."

"Huh?"

"Shouldn't you be finishing that up as fast as you can before too many boxes pile up?"

I stared at the counter space from where I had just taken my ingredients. It was already entirely covered by more supplies. We really would run out of room soon. *Whoops. I gotta get this done.*

As I returned to busily working away, Leo went to go get even more herbs.

In the end, I didn't get a chance to ask Leo what he'd been thinking about. It wasn't until the day of our departure for the slime wood that I found out.

ACT
4
Rematch

"**G**OOD MORNING, Sei!" Aira called out as she jogged over to me.

"Oh, Aira! Good morning."

Today was the day we would head for the slime wood. I was on my way to the rendezvous point as usual when I ran into Aira. I stopped and waited for her to catch up before we continued.

Aira smiled happily. "We'll be in the same squad today."

I smiled back. "Yup."

We'd both gone on tons of expeditions, but this was the first time we'd be going together, which made me happy for some reason.

Aira qualified for the slime wood expedition because of her skill in offensive magic. Specifically, in addition to Holy Magic, Aira could use Water and Wind Magic.

"You're going to be part of our offense today?" I asked.

"Yeah. I'm planning to keep an eye out and jump in when I can."

"What do you mean by that?"

"You and I are the only ones who can use Holy Magic, so I'm mainly on healing duty."

"Huh? But I thought Lord Drewes could use Holy Magic, too."

"The other mages told me he probably can't be counted on in that department." Aira smiled awkwardly.

"Ah." I totally understood. In Ghoshe Forest, Yuri had been pretty exclusively on the offensive.

If I use area-of-effect spells, I can probably handle all the healing on my own, but I'll run out of MP faster that way. It probably is best if Aira and I handle the healing together, I thought as we finally arrived at the square.

The other expedition squads were there, too, so the square was pretty busy despite it being so early in the morning. Everyone was grouped by destination, so Aira and I looked for people in our squad. We spotted a bunch wearing robes—the mages. That had to be Team Slime Wood.

"Aira, think that's us?"

"Mm-hmm."

We started over when I spotted Leo among the knights.

Upon closer inspection, several mercenaries were with him, too.

Huh? What are they doing here? I tilted my head inquisitively as I got sidetracked.

Leo noticed me as well and raised a hand. A few other folks noticed his movement and looked toward me.

"Good morning, Lady Sei!" several of them called in unison.

Whoa. That, coupled with their volume, left me a bit surprised. "Uh, good morning."

I wasn't the only one shocked either. Leo, his mercenaries, and Aira all wore astonished looks.

These men who greeted me in a boisterous chorus, wearing such radiant smiles, were the guys from the Second Order. Most of them looked somewhat familiar.

However, I was more concerned about Leo at the moment. I'd thought the mercenaries and the knights were back to acting separately.

"Good morning, Leo," I said.

"Hey—I mean, good morning, Lady Saint." Leo got all stiff under the sharp gaze of the knights of the Second Order.

"I told you, there's no need to be so formal with me.

I'd prefer you talk with me as a friend." When I said that, the Second Order guys relaxed. Thank goodness.

"By the way, what are you doing here, Leo?" I asked.

"We're with you guys today."

"You are?"

It turned out that at Lord Klausner's request, Leo and his men would be escorting us, too.

The slime wood had once been an area where dozens of valuable herbs grew, and it was the richest natural harvesting resource in Klausner's Domain. Upon hearing this section of the forest had been devastated by slimes, Lord Klausner had understandably wanted to dispatch Leo and his men as well. I suspected he wanted his mercenaries to be his eyes so they could see for themselves the state of the forest, especially since they would know what it had once looked like.

I also learned there had been some hiccups coordinating things between the knights and the mercenaries, so the company's participation had only been finalized the night prior. At first, Leo had been the only one assigned, but he had requested permission for some of his men to come, too. That had led to a bit of a dispute, which was why it had taken a while to come to a decision.

There had also been tiffs among the knights about who would be going to the slime wood even before the

Second Order arrived—I could only imagine the assignments had grown more complex after.

Thank you for your hard work in organizing everything, Albert, I thought.

"Morning, Sei."

"Good morning, Lady Sei."

Albert and Yuri joined us as I was talking with Leo. Seeing the two of them together was like staring into twin suns. I had to squint a little.

Aira and I said our good mornings as well. Yuri then glanced at Leo and tilted his head. "Who's this?"

"This is Leonhardt, the leader of the mercenary company in Klausner's Domain," I said.

"It is a pleasure to make your acquaintance," said Leo.

"He and some other mercenaries will be joining us today," Albert explained.

Yuri put on a friendly smile and nodded gracefully. "And I am Yuri Drewes, the grand magus of the Royal Magi Assembly. It's nice to meet you as well."

Leo's eyes widened in surprise. "Oh! Well, I look forward to working with you today."

"As do I with you."

The other mercenaries seemed somewhat flustered as well. They all straightened their posture, looking like they were standing at attention.

I guess Yuri has a pretty high position. But wait, doesn't Albert, too? Were they like this the first time they met him? I wondered.

But the truth came out relatively quickly. As Albert and Yuri walked away, I heard the mercenaries whisper among themselves.

"That's the Fiend of Embers!"

"Hey—keep it down."

"Fiend?" I asked, startled. That was a pretty alarming name to call someone!

"Oh, don't tell anyone about this, okay?" Leo whispered.

"But why would you call him that?"

Leo kept his voice lowered to explain. This fearsome "Fiend of Embers" was none other than Yuri himself. He had earned the epithet when he completely incinerated everything around him during a large-scale monster-slaying expedition some time ago. Several mercenaries had participated in that expedition, and Yuri had become something of a legend to everyone in the profession. They now watched him leave with equal amounts of fear and awe.

I heard them murmuring about how Yuri had unleashed a massive Fire Magic spell right before their eyes, all the while wearing that beautiful smile, illuminated by the flames in the midst of searing heat. When all was said and done, he had reduced everything before him to ash.

"What a perfect nickname," I muttered.

"Right?"

It made me want to call Yuri a fiend, too. Back in Ghoshe Forest, he'd gotten pretty hotheaded—but he'd limited himself to saying things, not acting on them. He really must have been holding himself back. Case in point: the western forest was still standing.

"What's that look for?" Leo asked.

"Oh, I was just thinking that I hope he uses some discretion this time, too," I said.

"What do you mean?"

"I hope the forest will be okay."

Leo grimaced. "You mean a repeat of that nightmare? You gotta stop him for me."

I couldn't help but be a little worried. Although we'd found a black swamp in Ghoshe, it had only produced a lot of monsters—it hadn't harmed the forest itself. Thus, Yuri had been motivated to leave the forest alone in order to preserve it.

Meanwhile, here in Klausner's Domain, the slimes had already withered a number of trees in the forest depths. The forest was injured, and parts of it were dying. I feared that upon seeing that the forest was in danger of no longer being a forest at all, Yuri would decide he could just let loose.

I agreed with Leo that this was the nightmare scenario and that it should be circumvented at all costs. In fact, the destruction the slimes had wrought was even more reason to avoid harming the forest any further—especially as there might still be some herbs growing in nooks and crannies, just barely hanging in there.

Yuri and I will be sharing a carriage, so I'll be sure to beg him to please, please, please restrain himself during the expedition. Yes, that's what I'll do.

With renewed determination, I made my way to the carriage.

"What do you think?"

"Uh, I think you have a good physique."

"Thank you!" The knight, who was so tall I had to strain my neck to see his face, beamed.

I didn't think my honest opinion necessitated thanks, but now some other knights looked at him enviously. Oh, come on, they all had nice physiques, too!

The first time I'd met Leo, I had been struck by his largeness, but the Second Order knights were his rivals in both height and...thickness. And by thickness, I meant pure muscle. While not thin by any means, compared to them, Albert looked slender, to say nothing of Yuri the reed. Perhaps by people who had a reputation for their defensive skills, Albert had actually meant those who were absolutely ripped?

"So, that's your type, huh?"

"Huh?" I asked without thinking.

The question had come from Leo, who now stood between me and the knight.

"Where'd that come from?" I asked him.

"You seem quite taken with Sir Knight here."

"I-I am not. I was just amazed by how *tall* he is."

"That so? There's plenty of knights in good shape around here."

"Yeah, but, tall's different."

"Oh, yeah?"

I was by no means drooling over their muscles. I was just thinking about how my friend back in Japan would be crying with joy if she were here right now.

"What's that? Boss, you wonderin' what kind of guys the Saint's into?" one of the mercenaries joked.

"Oh, has spring finally come for our boss?" another laughed.

"Huh? Get real," Leo snorted.

"You've been awfully interested in the Saint for a while now, if you ask me."

"Why you—stop your yammerin' and get vigilant! Keep an eye out already!"

The mercenaries crowed, entirely amused.

"Oh no, the boss is mad!"

"How scary!"

I think his men were just trying to pick on him. They all seemed to be on really good terms. Even though a vein throbbed in Leo's temple, he laughed them off. "Yeah, yeah, whatever."

We were only able to joke around like this while we walked because everyone was so good at their job. We went at a faster pace than we had the last time we'd moved through the forest—very expedient all around. One reason for that was that we had more people to take care of monsters, but the main reason was Yuri.

"There's one!" a mercenary at the vanguard shouted.

"At last. *Ice Spear.*" Yuri, also at the front, calmly dealt with the monster. A thick wedge of ice pierced through one of the creatures that looked like giant tropical pitcher plants. Dead in one hit.

Yup. We went so fast because every monster who dared to cross our path was dead in the blink of an eye thanks to Yuri. Even monsters that would have taken other mages multiple spells to defeat were felled by a single one of his. No surprise.

At present, despite my concerns, no harm had really come to the forest either. The extent of the damage was limited to that caused by any Wind Magic spells monsters managed to dodge—a few cut branches here and there. Yuri seemed to be taking care to choose spells with limited collateral damage. Maybe he'd actually been listening when I asked him to be thoughtful about it.

"Whoa. That was incredible!" one mercenary exclaimed.

"He killed it in one hit?" another replied, equally astonished.

The confrontations kept finishing before anyone even needed to ready themselves for combat. It was especially impressive to those who weren't used to seeing magic at work. Even I clapped the first time I saw Yuri take a monster out in one hit.

Meanwhile, the mages wore troubled looks.

"Um, is it really okay that we're not doing any fighting?" Aira asked a nearby mage.

The other mage was also frowning. "Not really, but..."

Despite that, the mages made no move to stop Yuri. Aira wore an increasingly familiar half-smile, half-frown.

Honestly, the mages probably couldn't stop their grand magus even if they tried. They seemed pretty resigned as they talked amongst themselves.

"If this were a normal expedition, we wouldn't be nearly as relaxed."

"Yeah. But it's always like this when you go with him."

"True. The one in Ghoshe got pretty intense, though."

"Even the grand magus seemed to be having trouble."

"There are only so many foes you can take on by yourself. You can't just mow down everything that comes at you if you're surrounded."

"I still feel like *he* might be able to."

"If he did, there wouldn't be any forest left."

The others groaned in agreement.

What a disquieting exchange. Were they referring to the same legendary expedition the mercenaries still talked about? In any case, I sincerely hoped we wouldn't see Klausner's forests burnt to the ground.

We continued at the same pace for a bit before we decided to take a rest. We would start running into the slimes soon, so the knights wanted to give us mages a break before we did.

We gathered in a glade and broke into teams so some people could rest while others kept a lookout before switching off. I thought I'd join in with my usual camp jobs, but the knights near me put down a folding stool and encouraged me to sit.

Everyone's still getting everything ready. Why am I sitting now? As I hesitated, one held out a hand to help me down, and that was that. I wouldn't get anywhere refusing him, so I gave up and took my seat.

"Thank you."

"Don't mention it!"

"Um, but shouldn't I help out?"

"Don't worry about that! You should rest here! You can count on us to do everything for you!" the knight responded, his eyes sparkling.

There's no way this guy isn't from the Second Order, I thought. *Maybe I should talk to someone about this? It feels kinda weird to just lounge about, twiddling my thumbs. Hmm, let's see...*

On one side of the encampment, I saw Albert talking to Yuri and some knights, looking preoccupied. Just then, Aira happened to pass by, so I called to her. She hesitated at first, but the mages nearby encouraged her, so she timidly came over.

The knights also put out a folding chair for Aira, so I gestured her down next to me.

"Good job so far today," I said.

"You, too. Though it's not like I've done anything," Aira replied.

"Me neither. I haven't even had any chances to heal."

"And I haven't had any chances to attack."

"It's amazing how quickly Lord Drewes dispatches the monsters we run into. He really is remarkable."

"Right?"

At least being with Aira made things less excruciating. Sitting around taking it easy by myself while everyone else did the heavy lifting made me feel guilty, but having an accomplice diminished the feeling. I did regret forcing Aira to be that accomplice, though.

As we chatted and giggled, we heard footsteps approach. I looked up to find Yuri walking toward us. Speak of the devil and all that.

"Good job out there."

"You, too."

It seemed Yuri had decided to take a break with us once he finished with Albert. I thought he'd sit, too, but he told me to hand over my traveling cup instead. I thought this odd but handed it over anyway. He filled it with water using magic.

"Here you are," he said, handing it back.

"Thank you." I looked at the contents and found ice

floating in it. Had he used some kind of spell that mixed both Water and Ice Magic? I was grateful for it whatever the case, being all sweaty from the walking.

Yuri did the same for Aira as well. Aira took the cup graciously and was surprised to find ice in hers, too. It was just ice, but even so, it was *ice*. Ice was valuable in Salutania, so anyone would have been surprised to so casually receive it.

After a moment, Aira looked up at him with curiosity. "Was that Ice Magic?"

I thought that rather mage-like of her, but then again, she was one of the Assembly now. Either way, Yuri's answer surprised her.

"Huh? You only used Water Magic?" she said.

"That's right. If you imagine the water in a frozen state while you cast, you can conjure it as such. At least, that's the gist."

"Water can become ice just by force of will?"

"Indeed. I found out while experimenting with the temperature of conjured water."

Aira asked one question after another, wearing an intently interested look. Yuri answered them all with a smile. Suddenly, he looked at me. "I came up with the notion after seeing your power at work."

"Wait, really?"

"Quite. You use the same magic to produce different effects, don't you?"

True enough, even before Yuri had seen me "practicing" with the Saint's magic in the fields a few days ago, he'd known that I had used the same power to alter the research institute's gardens to increase the effectiveness of our herbs. Both of those feats differed quite a bit from using the same power to purge the swamp in Ghoshe Forest.

I agreed that he had a point, which made his smile deepen. "I found Water Magic more malleable than, say, Fire Magic, and I did manage this much—though it requires a degree of channeling."

There it was again: channeling. The almighty channeling.

I wonder if Jude and Aira could both learn to make ice with their Water Magic? However, who knew how much control Yuri expended in order to pull that off?

He confessed that he still hadn't conducted any experiments to see whether people whose only elemental affinity was with Water Magic could also conjure ice. He knew that the extent to which fire, water, or ice could be conjured with simple spells increased with focus and will, but doing the same with more complicated magic was still a matter of hypothesis.

As we chatted, Albert came over to join us, several small pouches in his arms.

"Good work so far today," Aira and I said at the same time and chuckled at ourselves.

Albert sat next to me and handed me a pouch.

"Are these the cookies?" I asked him.

"That's right. I doubt we'll have a chance to rest again later, so we should probably eat these now while we have the chance."

"That's true. Thank you."

I thought I had recognized the pouch—it was full of the rosemary and walnut cookies I had made to be portable rations.

Albert also handed pouches to Aira, Yuri, and a nearby knight. We waited until Yuri was seated across from me before we opened our pouches and started eating. As I opened mine, I inhaled the hint of rosemary wafting up from it.

"Did you make these?" Aira asked.

"Mm-hmm. They're not very sweet, but I hope you like them."

"Wow! Thanks!" Aira picked a cookie and popped it into her mouth. Since it was so small, she got it in one. Aira smiled at the taste, which left me relieved.

"It's been a while since I last enjoyed something made by Lady Sei," Yuri said.

"I haven't been able to partake in her cooking nearly as often either," Albert said.

"Really? But you've been out here together for well over a month now."

"She's only been able to cook two or three times since we arrived. She can't always borrow the kitchens, after all."

"I suppose that makes sense."

Satisfied, Albert and Yuri tried their cookies, too. Albert had been my taste tester, and he clearly enjoyed them as much as usual. He didn't really care for overly sugary foods, though. But what about Yuri? He had a sweet tooth, so I feared he wouldn't find them palatable. As the creator of the cookies, I watched for his reaction on tenterhooks.

"How are they?" I asked after he swallowed.

"They're mild, as far as sweetness goes, but not bad if I think of them as a proper meal. The aroma of rosemary and walnuts accents them well. All in all, quite delicious."

Better than I thought! Thank goodness. Maybe it was Yuri's nature as an academic, but he didn't mince words when it came to giving his opinion.

Later, I learned the cookies were well received by others as well. A ton of knights and mages wanted to bring them along on future expeditions, too. That was that. I'd be making further adjustments to the recipe when I got back to the capital!

Although, while potions were one thing, I couldn't really justify making portable rations for everyone while

I was on the job at the institute. I would probably have to entrust the task to someone else. Either way, Albert told me we could discuss it more with Johan when we got back to the capital.

With that, everyone was refreshed, and we started back into the forest.

As we continued, we arrived at the slime wood. Once we started running into the slimes, the other mages finally got their chance to join the fray.

"Water Wall!" A wall of water sprang up to block a slime's venomous spray. The wall did its job, and just as it disappeared, a mercenary swung his sword, forcing the slime to retreat. Another mage flung an offensive spell to finish it off, and the battle was over.

"Good job, Miss!" The knight thanked Aira for her initial cast, which had blocked the slime's surprise attack.

Aira smiled back. "Thanks!"

Although it had been sudden, they had worked in perfect synchrony.

Now it was my turn. *"Area Protection."*

"Oh! Support magic."

"Thank you, Lady Saint!"

"Don't mention it!"

I had to recast the spell now and again since its effects wore off over time. In a game, I would have been able to see how much time remained on each cast, so it would have been far easier to time the next spell. I didn't have such convenient markers in this world, and I had no choice but to include myself under the auspice of its protection so I would feel when it started to weaken. Also, because there were so many of us, I needed to push the spell's area of effect to its limits in order to catch everyone.

Unlike the knights and mages, many of the mercenaries had never benefited from support spells before, so they got excited whenever I did it. Some of them thanked me every time. At first, it was a bit disconcerting to hear them keep calling me "Lady Saint," but I was starting to get used to it.

"We're running into more and more of them," Albert said.

"Yeah. It won't be much longer until we make it to the point where we had to turn back."

"From here on out, it'll be do or die."

I nodded and glanced over at Yuri, who stood a bit farther away. He gave me an inquisitive look, so I shook my head to let him know it was nothing urgent.

It was just that I kept thinking of our earlier retreat.

Was another horde of slimes waiting for us? Most likely. I trembled a bit just thinking of how *many* there had been. Although we had more mages now, it was still possible we wouldn't be able to take them on with regular offensive magic alone. It would be more effective to use area-of-effect spells. In short, it was increasingly less likely that I could feasibly ask Yuri to heed my earlier request to hold back.

The landscape had already turned grayer, more desolate. I saw no hint of herbs, no matter where I looked. But when all was said and done, human lives were more important than rare plants. And when push came to shove, Yuri could cast his spells much faster than I could use the Saint's magic. We would be fortunate if the forest fringe remained—we had to allow that we might lose its heart. I inwardly sighed as we got going again.

"Dammit! There's too many of them!"

"Don't break formation! That goes for you mercs, too!"

"You can count on us!"

Just as we predicted, when we arrived at the point where we had retreated before, we faced a great swarm of slimes all at once. The knights and mercenaries lined up in a semicircle around the mages and me. The mages flung offensive spells from behind as I stood ready to support.

Physical attacks didn't do much to the slimes, but the knights and mercenaries did enough with their blades to keep the slimes in check. They also literally used their bodies to shield us from venomous spray. While Healing Magic could cure wounds and status effects, we couldn't preemptively stop the pain they endured for our sake. Every fighter was injured while they protected us. My heart ached for them, and I devoted myself to healing their wounds.

"Sei!"

"Lord Hawke!"

As I cast a healing spell on a knight who had succumbed to a harmful status effect, a slime dropped from above. I had only just finished casting my spell, and in the midst of recovering my focus, I was slow to react. Albert shoved me aside, and while I was saved, he took the hit in my stead.

The slime coiled around Albert's right hand, and before my eyes, his skin started to melt away.

My magical power surged up within my chest—but someone put a hand on my shoulder to stop me.

"Not yet."

I turned to see Yuri. "Lord Drewes!"

"Fire Arrow!" Yuri's flaming strike landed a direct hit on the slime. The monster released Albert's hand and

flopped to the ground. Without pause, Yuri cast another spell, killing it instantly.

"Thank you," I gasped.

"Don't mention it. Now quickly, heal him."

"R-right. *Heal!*" I cast as swiftly as I could.

"Thanks," said Albert.

I had held my breath, but I let it out as his reddened skin recovered its normal color. Not a scratch remained.

"Lady Sei," Yuri said.

"Yes?" I looked his way to find he wore an expression I didn't normally see on him—a smile, yes, but a bit strained.

"It seems there are a few too many slimes for us to handle. Do you remember what you asked of me?"

"You mean to avoid harming the forest?"

"Yes."

"All right... I understand."

Before we departed, we had decided I would do my utmost to reserve the Saint's magic until we reached the black swamp. Any use of it required a tremendous amount of MP. On top of that, the greater its reach, the higher the cost. We didn't know how large the black swamp would be, and with our limited resources (i.e., me and only me), it would be best if I didn't expend unnecessary power on wiping out monsters only to reach the swamp and have nothing left.

Yuri had stopped me to ensure I didn't waste powerful magic on a single slime—it would have been inefficient. But if I was limited in my use of the Saint's magic to fend off monsters, we could only rely on Yuri to deal with them because of his ability to use area-of-effect spells.

However, casting one of those inevitably meant harming the forest. I was painfully reluctant to allow this, but in these dire circumstances, it would be selfish to ask him to keep avoiding actions that could save other people from harm. Therefore, I gave my consent. No need to hold back. Not anymore.

Once Yuri had my consent, it was all over in a whirlwind of magic. He mowed down swarms of slimes in a single blast—and those that still lived after his first salvo were picked off by the other mages.

Thanks to this, the knights and mercenaries were no longer forced to serve as shields, and I no longer had to use my MP healing their wounds and relieving them of harmful status effects. It hurt a bit, to think that I'd let them put up with so much pain. I should have let Yuri off the leash the second we reached the slime wood.

The farther we went, the more slimes we encountered. Soon there were so many it seemed like we faced an undulating sea of ooze. That was when we found the black swamp.

It began in a location where only a few dead trees remained, and it stretched out even farther than the one we had seen in Ghoshe Forest. I was speechless. *This isn't a swamp—it's a lake.*

We only had a few moments to waste gawping. Just like in Ghoshe, slimes started sliding out of the lake by the dozens—hundreds. We had to hurry.

"Keep them back!"

"Use barrier magic!"

"Ice Wall!"

"Earth Wall!"

Starting with Albert, the other mages cast their spells, and walls of ice and earth sprang out of the ground. The slimes that came at us from around the walls were cut down and forced back by the knights and mercenaries. We slowly made our way toward the swamp, but before we could get too close, the monsters came at us so fiercely that we couldn't make any more progress at all.

I wanted to use the Saint's magic and purge everything, but if we didn't get closer, the range I would need to cast would seriously drain my MP.

"Lady Sei, do you think you can purge the swamp from this position?" asked Yuri.

"If I have to—but we should get closer."

"Then allow me to pave the way."

It appeared Yuri had still been holding back. At least, that was what I thought upon seeing the next spell he cast.

"Inferno." A wave of flames roared forth all at once, enveloping a vast stretch of land before us. At the same time, the other mages cast a series of ice and water barriers in front of our group.

Good thinking! That'll mitigate the scorching wind coming back our way.

"Wow, that's amazing!"

"So this is the true power of the Fiend of Embers."

"It's been a while since we last got to see the grand magus's most powerful fire spell."

"Stop wasting time being impressed. We gotta keep pushing forward while we can."

"All right. Come on, people—let's cool the earth with water and ice."

The mages followed up with water and ice spells as they delivered the finishing blows to any surviving slimes. Steam billowed up everywhere, clouding our vision, so another mage used Wind Magic to blow it away and let us see.

We rushed ahead as soon as we knew the way was clear, and I concentrated on summoning up the Saint's magic. In moments, I felt the magical power flow forth from my chest. The power turned into a golden torrent, pouring from under my feet toward the swamp. There, it spread, filling the distance between the dead trees.

The slimes were purged the instant the magic touched them, fading into a black mist. However, this mist slowed the speed of my spell's expansion wherever they met, almost as if it was fighting my power.

Wider, farther—so that it'll cover the whole swamp. I folded my hands before my chest as if in prayer, extending my magical power as I envisioned the black mist washing away. *Please purge the monsters and the miasma.*

With that, the golden mist swallowed the entire swamp, and my spell set in. Every surface that had been blanketed by my magic sparkled, overtaking the black mist with purifying light until it faded away. Then the light burst, and after the last of the black mist vanished, golden sparkles fluttered down from the sky.

Everyone stared at the spectacle, awestruck and silent. All that remained were dead trees and naked earth.

ACT
5

Restoration

AFTER I PURGED the black swamp, we returned
to the village closest to the slime wood. As we had
to return from the depths of the forest, we didn't arrive
until close to sundown. We planned to stay there for two
nights, and once we recovered from the expedition, we
would head back to the capital of Klausner's Domain.

With the swamp gone, we saw no more monsters on
our way back than we had on the way in. We all felt a
sense of accomplishment for getting the job done, so the
air grew lively. Whenever we took a rest, everyone had
something to say about Yuri's area-of-effect spells or the
power of the Saint.

The knights from the Second Order, many of whom
had now seen my power up close for the first time, were
especially wowed. It felt like their impulse to idolize

me had skyrocketed, and soon they might actually get down on their knees and start worshiping the ground I walked on.

Please, I beg you, don't do that!

Although the journey itself was peaceful, I didn't feel that peace within. I was too haunted by the sight of the forest after I purged the black swamp. On our way in, the farther we'd pressed into the forest, the more dead trees we'd found, but around the swamp, even those had been few and far between. Once the swamp dissipated, the only thing left had been those few remaining trees and the barren earth—a forlorn scene, to say the least.

To hear others tell it, the forest depths had once overflowed with greenery and a bounty of invaluable herbs. It hurt my heart to see it reduced to a bleak stretch of absence, so different from the verdancy I had imagined.

Would the forest recover with time? It was probably just wishful thinking to imagine those same rare herbs would one day return to these woods. I hoped they would, at least...

"What's wrong?"

The question snapped me out of my reverie. Before I realized it, we had reached the village. I looked up to meet Albert's gaze. He frowned at me worriedly.

I shook my head. "Nothing really. I was just thinking."

His expression softened. "Are you sure? If you're tired, then maybe you should retire early."

"Thank you."

I didn't want to worry him. I would focus on just enjoying the feast. We would likely have a full-scale banquet when we got back to the capital of the domain, but for now we intended to throw a celebratory dinner party of sorts.

The village didn't have a large inn or dining hall, so while I called it a dinner party, it was more like we were all going to gather around a bonfire outdoors. Also, we paid for our own food and drink.

However, I helped make the food, so I think it became extravagant in its own way. The mercenaries hunted us some meat along the way, which was a big help as well. In the end, everyone praised the food, so I was gladdened to see my hard work make at least some difference.

"Sei?" Albert asked at one point during the night.

"Oh, sorry." I had tried to focus on the celebration, but the loss of the forest still weighed on my mind. I had sunk into thought again and worried Albert with my ruminating. The alcohol was probably a bit to blame for that. In any case, I was full, so I decided to call it a night. "I'm sorry. I think you're right. I probably should have retired early."

"All right. I'll walk you to your quarters."

Although I was turning in, the knights and mercenaries hadn't yet had their fill—they really had some impressive stamina. I would have felt bad making anyone break up the party before they were ready to go, so I planned to take care of myself. But now Albert was offering to leave early just for my comfort. That was chivalry for you.

It wasn't far to the house where I had been given a room, but unlike in Japan, the night was a frightful pitch-black. So, while I felt like an inconvenience, I gladly accepted his offer.

"Thank you," I said.

"Don't mention it."

We didn't speak as we walked. I think he wanted to let me mull things over. The silence didn't feel uncomfortable or anything. When we reached the door to my quarters, Albert stopped and turned to me. He was wearing that same soft expression.

"Thank you for walking me back," I said.

"It was my pleasure. Rest well tonight."

"Thank you... Um, wait." I stopped him just as he was about to walk away.

"Hm? What is it?"

"Um, if it's all right, there's something I'd like to do." This request felt like overstepping. At the same time, it just felt *wrong* to leave things as they were. So at last, I told Albert everything that had been on my mind all night.

The next day, I returned to the slime wood, though I was accompanied by far fewer people this time around.

Albert had given me permission to return to the forest after I explained what had been bothering me. However, this generosity came with a whole bushel of conditions, including this escort.

Everyone in the Kingdom of Salutania knew the Saint had the ability to purify miasma and exterminate monsters with her magic. However, hardly anyone knew the magic could do far more than that. Officials at the highest level of power in the Salutanian government had long since decided that the Saint's powers should be kept concealed and therefore had imposed a strict veil of secrecy around them. But today, I had returned to the forest because I hoped to use those powers for something other than the Saint's legendary purification.

Truth be told, I didn't know if it would work.

Given all that, I hadn't told Albert exactly what I hoped to do—I'd said something vague about wanting to try something out. He'd seemed to catch my drift, however.

Our party was small, but we arrived at our destination rather quickly. We stood at the edge of the unhealthy part of the forest where only the vestige of undergrowth and a handful of healthy trees remained. Soon, we would reach the barren stretch of earth where the black swamp had been.

"Just what are you planning to do?" Yuri asked as he walked beside me.

"Um, well, a little something."

He kept glancing at me with such anticipation in his eyes. My escort being so minimal, the grand magus was naturally among them. Granted, I got the impression that he would have followed me no matter who tried to stop him. I supposed that since this outing hinged on my magic, there was no avoiding him anyway.

When I knelt on the edge of the barren earth to concentrate on casting the spell, I felt his intent gaze fix upon me. It kinda bothered me to know he was staring at me like that, but I needed to focus.

Time dragged. My head wouldn't clear.

"Um..." I muttered.

"Yes?" said Yuri.

"Uh, um, it's just, your staring, it's, uh, it's bothering me."

I just couldn't concentrate! I knew Yuri was infatuated with my Saintly powers and all, but having him stare at

me so up close and personal like that was beyond unnerving. It felt like he was observing me even more closely than he did when I practiced my spells at the Royal Magi Assembly practice grounds.

"I apologize," he said. "I just can't help but wonder what exactly it is you need to do in order to summon this magic."

I jerked in surprise.

"Therefore, I thought that perhaps if I stud—I mean, witnessed you using the power, then I might gain new insight. We can learn quite a lot merely by observing a phenomenon, you see."

You were just about to say "studied," weren't you? Well, I'm not fooled by that smile of yours.

Days ago, he had let me off the hook and told me I didn't have to explain the secret to summoning the Saint's magic if I didn't want to—but how had it come to this? To be fair, I'd had an inkling that it would. No wonder I'd felt a chill in that moment. I'd had an unconscious premonition of this very future as Yuri's favorite lab rat. To think I had imagined that I'd dodged his bullet.

"If you would prefer to just tell me instead, that would be fine," he said.

"Uh, no, feel free to just observe what I do."

"Thank you."

I yielded, surrendered, gave up. I hadn't been able to tell him the truth when alone together in a private room; no way could I tell him when Albert stood mere feet away.

Okay, Sei, just do your best to ignore the piercing gaze boring into your side. I took a deep breath to settle myself and once more called up my focus. It was definitely just my imagination that my face felt slightly hot.

Slowly, almost as if turning back the clock, I recalled the moments I had shared with Albert. I thought of the night before when he had walked me home, and of healing him in the slime wood, and all the way back to the moment we had first met...

And the golden magic flowed forth from within my chest. It surged like a wave toward the blackened heart of the forest.

More. More... Normally, at some point I felt like I had reached my goal, but this time I just kept going and going. *Reach as far as possible...until the forest is brought back to life. That's my wish.*

Just as my head started to feel heavy, and my body trembled like it would fall over, I cast the spell.

"What the?!"

"Oh, my!"

The spell activated, and everything as far as the eye could see was bathed in a golden light. Within the illumination, a carpet of green burst forth and spread forward from my feet. The roots of dead trees sprouted anew and grew ever farther. It was like a video of a forest in fast forward, and it was wondrous to behold.

I couldn't make plants grow from nothing—but I could encourage the plants that had survived to take root where others had passed before them.

I'm so glad it worked... That was the last thing I thought. The urge to sleep overcame me, and I fell over, consciousness lost.

Apparently, after I lost consciousness, everyone panicked. Luckily, Yuri was instantly able to diagnose my condition: I had used every last drop of my MP. Thus, after a bit of time to recover, I woke back up all by myself.

However, when I came to, I was in Albert's arms. Yeah, I was flustered as heck. He was carrying me like some kind of fairy-tale princess! Of course I lost my mind a little!

I asked him to put me down right away, but he wouldn't, leaving me plenty perplexed.

Yuri peeked over Albert's shoulder with that beautiful smile to sing, "It's punishment for scaring us all half to death!"

After that, I didn't have the will to insist on anything.

In the end, I wound up getting carried that way for about ten whole minutes. It would have been longer, but my heart just couldn't take it anymore and I gave in to begging. That got Albert to finally let me down. In exchange, I wasn't allowed to do anything but rest once we got back to the village.

When I awoke the next morning, the preparations for our return to the capital were complete. I felt selfish for not helping, so along the way, I worked extra hard at cooking.

When we made it to the capital, I accompanied Albert, Yuri, and Leo to report that I had purged the black swamp off the face of the planet.

Lord Klausner looked a bit gutted when he first heard Leo describe what had happened to the forest near the swamp. I wanted to tell him it was okay, but as I had restored the forest with my Saint's magic in secret, Leo didn't know it had recovered, and I certainly couldn't say anything. I couldn't even tell Corinna, who was also receiving the report.

However, now that the swamp was gone, the number of monsters in the forest had dramatically decreased. We had experienced that firsthand on our return. I was sure that soon, Corinna would go to assess the state of the forest herself. I hoped so, at least. Then she would see the forest's recovery with her own eyes.

After we made our report, all that was left was to return to the royal capital. Just as I had predicted, Lord Klausner threw a banquet in our honor for the successful completion of our expeditions. It was to be a much bigger to-do than the feast we'd had back at the village. Being such a significant affair, that meant there would be a ton of things to do, right?

"Um, may I help get the banquet ready?" I asked him.

"You wish to?" Lord Klausner asked in surprise.

"Yes. May I help with the cooking?"

He looked even more surprised at that. But of course he would be. Even though I'd done it before, the idea of the Saint cooking was still outrageous to those of the kingdom. But I found it relaxing.

"I personally don't mind, however..." Lord Klausner trailed off, and his gaze shifted toward Albert.

My recipes had apparently spread far and wide throughout the kingdom, and they had also won over Lord Klausner's stomach. He and his family had only gotten to eat my cooking once, but it had been well received. Lord Klausner seemed tempted by a second opportunity to enjoy my cooking, but he looked to Albert because he had the final say on the matter.

I had already cooked for the Klausner clan once before, and I really hoped to be allowed to do it again. I looked pleadingly at Albert. *I'm sure that if I only cut vegetables and stuff like that, my Cooking skills won't have much effect. I promise I won't cook a whole recipe from top to bottom, so please, I'm begging here!*

He thought it over with a slightly consternated look, but then he glanced at me and sighed. "I don't mind either."

"Thank you!" I said. *And the victory goes to Sei!*

After we finished up our report, I took that permission as license to head straight for the kitchens. The chefs had already heard I was coming, and the head chef was there to greet me when I arrived. "What do you plan to make today?"

"Oh, nothing. I was thinking of helping out with mise en place and stuff."

"Is that so?" The chef looked disappointed.

"Well, I figured you already had a menu prepared for tonight, right?"

They obviously did. A ton of vegetables and other ingredients were laid out on the counters and were already being prepared. Those had to be for the banquet.

I definitely didn't want to ask them to change a menu they'd already started on.

However, it seemed the head chef really wanted to take advantage of the opportunity to learn something new. The other chefs also had expectant looks on their faces. Well, now I had no choice. I asked them to tell me what they'd already been planning to make, and I thought over what they could change or what things we could use for alternative recipes.

Luckily, they had some extra ingredients—enough to add one more dish to the banquet. I told them which ingredients we would need and that I would teach them the steps, and the chefs readily agreed with smiles on their faces.

We would make mutton leg and lentil stew.

As I cut up the carrots and onions, someone unexpected came to the kitchens.

"Aira?"

"I heard you were here, so I decided to stop by," she said. "I'd like to help, too."

Yuri had told her what I was up to. Aira got permission from the head chef to join in and came over to me. She told me she had cooked once in a while back in Japan. She had been living at home with both her parents, but since both of them worked, at times she'd had to make her own lunch and so forth.

"You made your own bento for school, huh? That sure brings me back. What kind of foods did you make?" I asked.

"Just simple things like scrambled eggs and fried sausages."

"Even so, I think that's pretty impressive."

We had a lot of vegetables to chop, since this was for a whole banquet. Aira and I had fun chatting about other food we used to eat back in Japan as we worked.

Eventually, I noticed we were the only ones talking; no one else joined in our conversations. I suspected it was because we were talking about food the chefs had never heard of before, so they were all listening with intent interest.

After we finished the mise en place, we got to the actual cooking. Only the chefs would be doing this part. I could have asked Aira to help, but I decided not to, just in case. I had never heard Aira talk about something like this, but there was a nonzero chance her Cooking skills might also have unusually impressive effects.

Following my directions, the chef fried the seasoned meat in a pan. At the same time, another chef sauteed the chopped vegetables in a big pot. Once they were cooked, we added the lentils and meat to the pot with the vegetables, as well as premade bouillon, and let it simmer for a good long time.

To add flavor, I used spices such as galangal and hyssop, which were a bit unusual even back in Japan. But the alchemist's holy land was well named indeed. I had found these in the brewery and asked Corinna how to get the herbs in the royal capital, as they could also be used as cooking spices.

"That was so fun. It's been a while since the last time I got to cook," Aira said.

"Yeah. If you'd like, you could come cook with me sometime when we get back to the capital."

"Really? I'd love to!" Aira nodded, beaming.

Aira had been dissatisfied with the cuisine in this world, too. She had been relieved when she started to get better tasting food in Klausner's Domain. I suspected that since she had been living an otherwise perfect life in the palace, she had been afraid to complain about the food and just tried to put up with it.

While I chatted with Aira, the head chef came over to tell us the stew was ready for a taste test. It was absolutely delicious. Mission accomplished.

After that, I headed back to my quarters. There, I found Mary and the other maids waiting for me. As this would be a significant banquet, I was expected to wear something Saint-like.

Noooo, again?

People of noble status had to dress according to the occasion, which meant that as the Saint, I had to dress up, too. And that meant proper grooming first. I had completely forgotten how troublesome the whole ordeal could be.

When Mary told me it was time to change, I wearily gave in—but when I saw the happy smiles on the other maids standing by, I promised myself that I would do as she said. They were really nice smiles, okay?

The maids seemed to enjoy dressing me up. They even asked if I would let them handle more of the preparation than I usually did. Most times, I did whatever I could on my own so they wouldn't have to work. Thinking back on it, I felt a bit sorry—they just wanted to show off their skills and feel useful, after all.

After the primping, they brought out yet another new robe for me. The cloth was the color of young herbs, and the dark green embroidery looked like vines. It reminded me of the branches and leaves that had burst back to life after I used my magic on the barren depths of the forest.

I was genuinely touched—it was so kind of the maids to prepare this kind of dress for me. *I'm sorry! I just can't handle corsets.*

The maids showered me with praise when their work was completed.

"And...finished."

"You look beautiful."

"Truly."

I got pretty self-conscious. I still wasn't used to this! However, I thought demurring or saying "oh, that's not true" would just downplay their skills, so all I actually said was, "Thank you."

They told me that my escort would arrive when it was time, so I sat about and chatted with the maids while I waited.

A little while later, there was a knock at the door. I couldn't say I was surprised to see that my escort would be Albert.

"You look lovely tonight," he said as he smiled.

"Oh, you're just saying that." I couldn't look him in the eye and reflexively stared down at my feet.

Ahhh, and here I'd told myself to be honest about the maids' skills! I was just so flustered. I glanced at the maids, mortified, but they were smiling at me fondly. Well, that just made me all the more flustered.

While I was trying to get a hold of myself, Albert chuckled and offered me his arm. "Shall we go?"

"Huh? Oh, yes." At first I wasn't sure what he was doing. *Oh, right, escort.*

I placed my hand on his elbow.

"Have a pleasant evening, my lady," said Mary.

"Thanks, see you all later!"

Mary and the other maids saw me off with precisely proper bows as I left the room.

Knights, mages, and mercenaries had already filled the banquet hall by the time we got there. Long tables were laden with food and alcohol. Of course, the stew Aira and I had made was laid out with the rest.

Albert guided me to the back of the room, to the table where the Klausner family was seated. The Klausners had the left side of the table, starting from the center. The seats on the right side of the table were empty, which I guessed meant they were ours.

Yuri had the seat farthest on the right. He noticed us enter the hall and raised a hand in greeting. We joined him in our assigned seats, Lord Klausner gave a speech, and at last the banquet began.

Lord Klausner thanked me again just as I took a sip of wine from a silver goblet. "Lady Sei, thank you for all you have done for my domain."

"I'm just happy I was able to help. And I would like to thank you as well. I learned so much while I was here."

Although I had come to give support for the expeditions, I had been able to study potions in the alchemist's holy land, so I was powerfully grateful myself. Plus, while it would take some time for Klausner's Domain to export herbs at the volume they once had, they had vowed to prioritize selling herbs to the research institute for me. I felt kind of bad, because it felt like they were going out of their way to be nice to us.

Albert thanked Lord Klausner for his offer all the same. That made sense, since he and his knights got their potions from the institute.

While we talked with the head of the table about the future, other people started digging in to the food. I heard delighted responses rise up from tables across the hall. Ah, this was the best—and most relieving—part of cooking.

The praise was particularly boisterous from the mercenaries' table.

"This is the food the capital's been raving about?" one asked.

"Holy—this is mind-blowingly good!" Leo exclaimed.

"Hey, Boss! Don't hog it all for yourself!"

"Shut up! It'd be poor manners not to eat this as fast as I can."

I looked toward the excited voices to see Leo hoarding the stew on his table. I couldn't help but laugh.

I wasn't the only one amused by the banter. Aira, sitting with the other mages, laughed joyfully.

Thank goodness. Those unfamiliar spices had done their job. Everyone vied to get a second helping of our stew.

At the end of a wonderful meal, I retired to my chambers early. I feared people couldn't properly enjoy themselves while the high-ranking folks were staring down at them from the head table. Maybe that was just the knights, though. The mercenaries didn't really seem to mind either way.

My hypothesis was right on the money. I heard from some of the Third Order knights that the party got even more raucous after we left.

Two days after the banquet, it was time to return to the royal capital. Those days passed in the blink of an eye. As I left the great hall, I found it hurt my heart a bit to be leaving the mercenaries whom I had gotten to know so well.

"Thanks for everything you've done for us," Lord Klausner said when I was saying my goodbyes to him with Albert.

"I should be the one thanking you for letting me learn so much from the alchemists in your brewery."

Corinna then arrived to say goodbye as well. She wasn't the only one either. A ton of people had come to see us off even though it was terribly early in the morning.

"We're going to have a hard time making potions without you around," she said to me.

"Oh, I hardly did anything."

"As if. You're the only one who can pump out potions like that. How many alchemists do you think it'd take to match your daily quota?"

I laughed bashfully. Corinna was the same as always, even when saying goodbye.

As I chuckled, she beckoned me to lean down. Now what was this about? "Thank you for what you did with the fields as well," she whispered. "I'm sure we'll be able to grow all manner of herbs again."

"To tell the truth, I was thinking I'd like to try growing those herbs at our research institute as well."

"Well, then. I'll send you some seeds in a bit."

"Thank you!"

Yay! Now I could also grow those finicky herbs that required blessings. Those seeds had been the one thing I still needed. My mind was in full-on victory pose as I thanked her. Corinna responded with a somewhat exasperated smile.

As we spoke in hushed tones, Leo strode over as well. He greeted me with his usual "Heya!" and a raised hand, so I gave him a slight bow in return.

"Time for you to head back?" he asked.

"That's right."

"Take care on the way then."

"Thank you. You take care of yourself, too, Leo."

"Thanks. But listen, if you ever get tired of the royal capital, you come back here, all right? You're always welcome to join us."

"What are you talking about?" Corinna cut in. "If she wants new work, then I've got dibs."

I wasn't planning on quitting the research institute, but if I did, then I supposed I could join the brewery instead. I found myself seriously considering it as a second career—I had enjoyed my time here in Klausner's Domain even more than I had anticipated.

As I listened to Corinna and Leo quarrel like some kind of comedy routine, I felt a bit wistful. It was possible that this would be the last time I saw them. We hadn't been in Klausner's Domain all that long, but I had grown utterly fond of these two.

"Sei, it's time." Albert urged me into the carriage.

"All right." I swallowed my emotions to say my final goodbyes to Corinna and Leo, then headed toward the carriage.

After I got in, it wasn't long before someone gave the order for departure. The carriage slowly began to roll forward.

When I looked out the window, I found Corinna, Leo, and the other mercenaries waving us off. I continued waving back until I could no longer see them. It was time at last to leave.

The Saint's Magic Power is Omnipotent

Short Story
COLLECTION

The Saint's
Magic Power is
Omnipotent

Valentine's Day at the Research Institute

I ADDED BUTTER, sugar, eggs, flour—and last, the most important ingredient—then mixed them together. Not all at once, mind you. I followed the steps in the recipe exactly, at least as far as I remembered it. You're bound to mess up sweets if you don't use the right quantities or if you get creative with the directions.

When I first got to Salutania, I had surprised everyone by using herbs in cooking. But one ingredient I used in these confections had originally been medicine itself. Where I came from, it was said to preserve youth and increase longevity. In other words, cacao: one of the ingredients for making chocolate.

They already sold chocolate here in the royal capital. When I saw it, I had been delighted. I knew that since they had chocolate, they had to have cocoa, too.

Thus, today I was using cocoa to make brownies.

Several seasons had come and gone since my summoning, but I was pretty sure it was now February back in Japan. That made me remember a certain event that took place every year, and I suddenly craved chocolate.

I had to make something.

While I'd never had a boyfriend as a student, I had made chocolates every year to give to friends. I knew how to pour the mixture into a mold, stick it in the oven, and wait.

I passed the time by leisurely reading a book. I became immersed in its world for a lovely little while, until a sweet fragrance began to tickle my nose.

Maybe it'll be ready soon? I opened the door to the oven to find the treats looking nicely baked. I took them out and placed them on the oven to cool.

"What are you making today?" Jude asked; he had been drawn in by the smell. He peered curiously at the brownies. "Are they burned?"

It must have been his first time seeing such a cocoa-rich confection.

"Nope," I said. "This is what they're supposed to look like."

"Huh."

I guess they might *look burned if you don't know better— but come on, do they smell burned to you?*

"I guess you just messed up the look, then," Jude continued.

"Say that again and you can't have any."

"I was just kidding, okay? I'm sorry," Jude apologized quickly. He actually had quite the sweet tooth, so much so that he was always first in line to taste test my new cookies and other treats.

Although, he always came after my taste testing with the other cooks.

I thought the brownies would taste better cooled, but Jude didn't look willing to wait, so I cut a piece from the edge. I mean sure, it smelled good, but how did it taste? I popped the piece into my mouth. Would it be as delicious as I remembered?

"Want to try it?" I had baked this by myself, so I had none of my usual assistants. I wanted someone else's opinion, too. Lucky for Jude!

He nodded happily. I looked for a plate to give him a slice, but he just opened his mouth.

Huh? What, does he want me to feed him? I chuckled nervously, resigned to his enthusiasm, and popped the piece in his mouth.

After a moment of chewing, a smile spread across his face.

"Do you like it?" I asked, and he nodded rapidly.

Thank goodness!

Not long after, Johan showed up. "Cooking again today, I see."

"It's not done yet, but would you tell me what you think, too?"

"Sure." Johan was another regular taste tester of mine. He let me put a piece on a plate for him, but when I went to hand it to him, he grinned. "What? You're not going to feed me, too?"

"What? You saw that?!" My face flushed with embarrassment.

He had walked into the kitchen just as I popped the piece into Jude's mouth. He hadn't wanted to interrupt, so he'd just waited in silence to pounce.

I wish you had just walked away! I glared at him. He laughed as he patted me on the head.

Valentine's Day with the
Knights of the Third Order

THE FINISHED BROWNIES had been taste tested by my coworkers and been well received. Jude even had two pieces—one for him and one for his sweet tooth. Johan did, too, for that matter.

I thought they'd come out pretty good, so I took some of the brownies over to the barracks of the Knights of the Third Order. I was a bit worried, though, since Albert wasn't fond of sweets.

"Please pardon my intrusion," I said as I entered the office of the knight commander.

As usual, Albert stood from his seat to greet me. Then he invited me to sit on one of the two sofas that faced each other.

"I heard from Johan that you've been working on some kind of new confection," Albert said as soon as I sat down, which surprised me. I had only made the brownies the day before. News sure traveled fast.

"I saw Johan last night," he told me with a wry smile. "He bragged all about getting to test it."

Somehow, I could perfectly imagine this scenario. *That man...* I let out an exasperated chuckle.

Just then, someone knocked on the door. The maid waited for Albert's response before coming in with tea. I came here only occasionally for teatime, but they always served it so quickly. The knight standing guard at the door must have summoned her.

After receiving the tea, I poured it into cups and placed the brownies on plates beside them on the table.

Albert smiled at the sight of the lovely spread. "So you did bring me some."

"Mm-hmm. I know you don't really love sweets, but I hope you enjoy it."

"You're right that I don't have much of a sweet tooth, but Johan made me curious."

"Is that so?"

"In fact, if you hadn't brought this here today, I was planning to drop by the institute tomorrow."

What?! He wanted to try them that badly? My eyes widened. I couldn't say I wasn't surprised.

Then Albert gave me a smile sweeter than any brownie.

Don't do that! You'll make me blush! I averted my eyes in an attempt to calm my pounding heart and sat on the sofa again.

However, after I did that, I didn't hear Albert's usual invitation to drink. I tilted my head in curiosity.

The moment our eyes met, he opened his mouth. I froze, confused. He smiled mischievously. "I heard that when you let your coworker taste it, you fed it to him."

"What?!"

I knew exactly what he was talking about! That Jude, opening his mouth so I could feed him like some kind of baby bird! And Johan had seen the whole thing. Johan had told Albert *the whole thing*.

And hey, Jude was one thing, but how could it possibly be proper to hand-feed a noble like Albert?!

"U-um, wouldn't that be a terrible breach of etiquette?" I asked.

"In a public space, yes. But it's just the two of us. It's fine."

"I-I see."

He said that with such anticipation written all over his face that I had no choice. I worked up my courage and popped a brownie into his mouth.

The Saint's
Magic Power is
Omnipotent

Escaping the Summer Heat: Lord Smarty-Glasses

I T WAS *hot*. Even though it was now autumn, it felt like summer during the day.

I was wearing a straw hat to protect myself against heatstroke and riding in a wagon pulled by a donkey, headed for the Royal Magi Assembly. I had a potion delivery to make. You see, after hearing my potions were fifty percent more effective, Yuri had given me a personal request.

I arrived at his office, knocked on the door, and entered the room. "Pardon me for the intrusion."

Although I received permission to enter Yuri's office, I didn't find the grand magus but rather Lord Smarty-Glasses.

Huh. Can I hand these over to him instead?

"I'm here to deliver the potions Lord Drewes requested," I explained.

Lord Smarty-Glasses nodded slightly and pointed. "You can put them there."

The manservant who had accompanied me carried the wooden box of potions to the designated location. Meanwhile, I handed the statement of delivery to Lord Smarty-Glasses, and he examined the numbers to ensure they checked out.

I gazed around the room while I waited, and a droplet of sweat ran down my cheek that dripped all the way to my chin. Although the window hung open, no wind blew through it, so the room was stifling. Granted, it did feel a bit cooler given the absence of direct sunlight.

Boy, do I miss air-conditioning... I wiped my sweat away with a handkerchief, and my eyes suddenly met Lord Smarty-Glasses's. Although I was drenched, he, who by all rights should've been roasting in that robe of his, didn't look the least bit sweaty. How was he so okay?!

"Aren't you hot?" I accidentally let the question slip the moment it popped into my head—I couldn't help it! My brain was too muddled by the heat. Regret, regret, regret.

But he didn't seem the least bit bothered. "I am not."

"Really?"

"You're not carrying an enchanted item?"

"Like what?"

Wait, was that what kept him cool? I looked questioningly at him, and he took off the pendant he wore. It had a simple design, and a blue-gray stone was embedded in it. He handed it over to me. "Put it on."

I did so without hesitation. Instantly, the hot feeling all over my body vanished as if it had never been there to begin with. A faint wave of cold air draped gently over my entire being. It was like someone had blasted an air conditioner directly at me and immediately dropped the humidity index in my vicinity.

"This is amazing! I feel so much better already."

"Is that so?" Lord Smarty-Glasses smiled faintly at my surprise. "You can keep it, if you'd like."

"Are you sure?"

"I don't mind."

He explained then that since he had an affinity for Ice Magic, he could just use his own magic to keep himself cool. He didn't really need any items for that purpose. He had just kept the pendant for convenience's sake. I worried that meant it would be an *in*convenience for me to take it, but he handed over the signed statement of delivery as if to say the conversation was over.

All right, but doesn't this cost a ton? I wondered, but Lord Smarty-Glasses had returned to his work. I lost my battle with temptation. I just felt so much more comfortable now! In the end, I kept the pendant when I headed back to the institute.

"Hmm? Where'd you get that pendant from?" Johan asked when I returned.

"Magus Hawke gave it to me."

"Huh?" Johan was surprised.

I told him the story, which just made him look even more astonished. Sure, I had also been surprised that Lord Smarty-Glasses handed over an enchanted item so casually, but not as flabbergasted as Johan looked right now. Was there a reason for that? I couldn't think of one.

At any rate, thanks to the pendant, I would be able to spend the rest of the summer feeling nice and cool.

I should thank him later, I thought, leaving the frozen Johan to return to my work.

Escaping the Summer Heat: Grand Magus Yuri Drewes

"I'D KILL FOR some shaved ice right now." I was in the middle of training at the Royal Magi Assembly practice grounds, but it was so miserably hot that I accidentally let that slip.

"Shaved ice?" Yuri gave me a curious look.

Shaved ice was famous in Japan, but they didn't have it in the Kingdom of Salutania.

"It's a kind of food we ate a lot during the summer where I come from."

"What's it like?"

"It's ice that's been flaked until it's all crunchy and soft, with fruit syrup on top."

"Shaved ice..."

Since ice was a luxury here, no desserts used it. For that reason, Yuri couldn't imagine what exactly shaved ice looked like, and he started asking me all sorts of questions about it. Unsurprisingly, I didn't really know how a shaved ice maker worked, so I could only tell him what I remembered in the vaguest sense. However, he at least seemed to get some kind of picture in his head.

After mulling this over for a bit, he cast an ice spell. A towering icicle jutted into the sky. I stared at this spike, which was taller than me, and then stared at Yuri, utterly bewildered. He was in the middle of casting a wind spell. It began to shave down the icicle before my very eyes.

"Would it work something like this?" he asked.

"Yeah, kinda."

The shaved ice mountain looking so stately there on the practice grounds that it left me gobsmacked. Cold air wafted off it in waves. I was beyond impressed that Yuri had been able to conjure and recreate shaved ice based on my shoddy explanation.

"Now you'd be able to make it so long as you had syrup, right?" Yuri asked.

"I suppose so."

"Then let's go!"

"Huh?" Now it was my turn to give him a curious look. *Go where? If it's syrup we're after, then maybe the institute's dining hall?*

Before I knew it, I'd followed a smiling Yuri all the way

to the palace kitchens. The chefs peered at Yuri's sudden appearance with due suspicion. Thankfully, I spotted someone who worked at the institute's dining hall among the chefs. She noticed me as well and came running over to us.

"May we help you?" she asked hesitantly.

"Can we borrow some space here?" Yuri asked. "There's something we want to make."

"Is that so?"

"Yes. Also, do you have fruit syrup or anything of the sort?" I asked. "I'd like to use that."

Perhaps it was because the chef had cooked with me at the institute before, but despite our sudden arrival, she let us borrow a corner of the kitchens. "Will this spot suit your needs?" she asked after she guided us over to it.

"Yes, thank you."

Another chef brought over several syrups as well as some jams. At Yuri's directions—and mine—we also received dishes and other implements I thought we'd need.

Once everything was ready, Yuri cast the same spells again. This time, he made a much smaller icicle appear on a large dish, then he shaved it down to make a miniature shaved ice mountain. I scooped the shaved ice into a smaller bowl, added syrup, and took a bite with a spoon.

Yeah, this is it! This frosty sweetness is to die for.

After I tasted it, I made a bowl for Yuri and passed it to him.

Eyes full of anticipation, he closely inspected the shaved ice before scooping up a spoonful and putting it in his mouth. His eyes widened in surprise, and a smile bloomed across his face. "My, my. Now this is a splendid treat for hot weather."

"Exactly. I always get a craving for it when summer comes around."

"I can see why."

The two of us ate our way through the rest of the shaved ice in completely satisfied silence. In the midst of this, Yuri noticed the chefs watching us and gave them permission to join in. They got their own bowls to try as well. Some of them voiced their surprise with great delight.

"Ah, that was so good." I sighed happily. It had been too long since I last enjoyed this.

I bet the heat's not going away anytime soon. I wish I could have this at least one more time. But it'll probably be hard to get this much ice again. I was so lucky that Yuri was interested enough to conjure some with magic.

"Thank you for the ice," I said.

"Don't mention it. I was all too pleased to try a new dessert."

"I'm so grateful I got to eat that treat again. It's been so long."

"If you ever want it again, I'll conjure as much ice as you like."

"Really?!" I asked excitedly.

Yuri covered his mouth with his hand and looked away, his shoulders trembling.

Huh? Is he laughing at me? I felt like our usual dynamic had been flipped on its head. But I couldn't help it— I really wanted to eat shaved ice!

The Saint's
Magic Power is
Omnipotent

Escaping the Summer Heat:
Knight Commander Albert Hawke

O NE DAY, Albert invited me to go back into the capital. Apparently, there was to be a festival of sorts. I had been to the city with him once before, so I thought it might be fun to go again and eagerly accepted.

The festival would be at night, so we would depart after I finished work. During the day, I learned the researchers were also planning to visit the festival as a group. When I remembered my last trip into the city with Albert, I elected to go with the my colleagues and meet with him there. I desperately wanted to avoid an anxiety-ridden round two of being knee-to-knee in a cramped carriage.

The few days before the festival passed in a flash, and all too soon, I packed myself into a carriage with my colleagues, and we were off.

Once we arrived, my colleagues waited with me at the designated meeting point—a crossroad just a bit away from the heart of the festivities. They considered it too dark for me to hang around all on my lonesome. I probably would have been all right, but if something did happen, what would I have done about it? I accepted their companionship without complaint.

Besides, I didn't have to bum around forever or anything. Albert showed up moments after we arrived. We had agreed to meet there because it would be so crowded everywhere else, but he wore exactly the same sort of clothes he had on our last visit to the city, so I spotted him right away.

"Did I keep you waiting long?" he asked.

"Not at all, we just got here."

After seeing me safely handed off, the researchers quickly disappeared into the crowd. Albert and I headed into the thick of the festival ourselves.

Right as we started off, he casually took my hand in his. Ohhh, nooo—I couldn't escape from the fact that we were walking while *holding hands*. And it wasn't just that either—he had to go and entwine his fingers with mine!

I looked up at him in surprise. He had the audacity to smile sweetly at me. "Something the matter?"

"No..."

Part of me still wanted to let go, but I couldn't now, not after he looked at me like that.

Eep... Just focus on everything else around you and forget about the hand. Yeah, that'll do it! Luckily, the sights of the city were so lively that I had plenty to occupy myself with.

Food stalls lined either side of the road leading up to the heart of the festival. The market I had visited before had sold fruits, vegetables, and the like, but most of the stalls tonight hawked street food that was ready to eat. Groups of wooden crates were arranged in front of the stalls. People sat on them to eat the food they had purchased.

Some people with reddened faces drank deep from their cups. That was alcohol for you. There had to be stalls selling that as well.

"Something catch your eye?" asked Albert.

"I was just wondering where people are getting their drinks."

"Do you have a taste for alcohol?"

"A bit."

I hadn't drunk anything alcoholic since my summoning, but that didn't mean I abstained by habit. I had gone drinking with friends back in Japan. I just hadn't yet had the chance in the kingdom. This being a festival, I thought a bit of alcohol might help get me in the mood.

After this, Albert brought me to a stall selling alcoholic beverages. I assumed it was ale, given the color, but the contents of the mug I received didn't smell like I expected.

"What's this?" I asked.

"Mead."

Mead, huh? I lifted the mug to my face again and took another sniff. It had a pleasantly sweet aroma, probably due to a lighter fermentation process. Either way, it sure tasted good, no question.

I sat on one of the crates like everyone else and took a few more sips. Before I knew it, food had been brought out for us as well.

Although the mead's alcoholic content was low, it was still, you know, alcoholic. As I drank, I gradually started to feel that familiar fuzzy warmth. As I grew light-headed, I ate and sipped while chatting with Albert about the festival and any other thing that occurred to us.

It really was a wonderful time—I know because it passed in the blink of an eye. Soon it was pretty late, so Albert suggested we head back to the palace.

By then, I was in such a good mood that I swung our linked hands and practically skipped all the way back to where the carriage awaited us. Albert chuckled merrily beside me.

Then, of course, I had to go and trip on a cobblestone—but Albert wrapped his arms around my waist to stop my fall. I think? It got a little hazy there at the end.

Needless to say, the next morning, I was left feeling powerfully flustered when I remembered that string of events.

The Saint's*
*Magic Power is *
Omnipotent

The Alluring Mushroom

FALL IS A GREAT SEASON for playing sports or holing up to read, but most of all, it's the season of food. Aside from it being the time when the fields are harvested, you can also gather all sorts of delicious food in the wild. At least, that was how it had been in Japan, and it turned out to be the same in the Kingdom of Salutania.

According to Jude, fall wasn't just the time for harvesting rye and other agricultural products—you could also gather all kinds of berries and mushrooms in the forest.

I gasped in delight when I heard. So where did I go next? The forest, of course.

I got permission from Johan without delay and set off for the forest east of the capital. I brought Jude and two other researchers with me, along with two knights from the Third Order to be our escort.

Once we got there, we moved as a group. We left it to the knights to keep an eye on our surroundings while the rest of us focused on looking for herbs. As we searched, I also found berries and mushrooms, which were my real objective. Just as you'd expect from harvest season, I found a lot more of both than I had on our previous visit.

While I was picking, I spotted something curious. As soon as I squatted down to pick a nearby herb, I saw a mushroom inconspicuously growing in the shadow of a fallen tree. It was short, stout, and had a faint beige color. I couldn't immediately tell whether it was safe to eat.

In such cases, it's always best to ask.

I called Jude over and pointed at the mushroom. He frowned at it suspiciously, then his eyes widened and he stared at me. I reflexively leaned back from the force of his stare.

"Wh-what is it?"

Jude's finger trembled as he pointed. "I-It's a..."

His weird behavior attracted one of our colleagues. But the second they looked where he was pointing, they let out a cry of surprise and paled.

What in the world was going on?

"Is there something weird about this mushroom?" I asked.

Jude nodded vigorously before launching into an excited explanation.

The thing I'd found was known as a shadow mushroom. It was indeed edible and known for its delicious taste, but its aroma was even more famously appealing. We couldn't smell it while it was growing, but once we cut it up, its fragrance would become clear. Some people even claimed that its aroma was so alluring that it could be used as an aphrodisiac.

Also, shadow mushrooms were so rare that they were also known as mystic shrooms. In fact, they were so uncommon that some said you could live ten lives and only hope to find one once. Furthermore, on account of that rarity, they could be sold for a fortune.

"Do you think Johan will tell us to sell it if we bring it back?" I asked.

"I doubt it. You're the one who found it, so he'll definitely let you do whatever you want."

Really? I thought Jude just sounded that confident because the mushroom was so valuable that he couldn't even predict how Johan would react, so he'd looped back around to certain.

But given everything I had just heard, I really didn't want to sell it—I wanted to *eat* it. My bet was that Johan would choose the same in my position. Even though he was our boss, he was still a researcher at heart. He'd definitely prefer to learn what this incredible rarity tasted like for himself.

With confidence, I picked the shadow mushroom.

When we got back to the institute and told Johan, he was as shocked as we thought he'd be. The next words out of his mouth were: "All right, let's see what it tastes like."

That made me burst out laughing.

He didn't let us down, either. We went straight to the dining hall and presented the mushroom to the chefs. They all stared and pointed, just like Jude had. It really was a once in a lifetime find. When I declared we wanted to cook it, they cheered.

I wasn't familiar with this kind of mushroom, so I asked the chefs for advice before deciding what to make. Because we wanted to celebrate that fantastic fragrance, I elected to chop it up and use it to garnish a complementary dish.

I let a chef take care of prepping the shadow mushroom as I worked on devising the perfect accompaniment. Finally, I settled on chicken in a white sauce stew.

I sliced and sauteed onions and more run-of-the-mill mushrooms, and then let them simmer with the cooked chicken in a white wine. We unfortunately didn't have heavy cream, so instead I added flour, milk, and butter.

I didn't forget to season it all with a moderate amount of salt and pepper, too.

At last, I scattered the pieces of shadow mushroom across the finished chicken, and the dish was ready.

Yup. It smelled mind-blowingly good. The moment we started chopping the shadow mushroom, an exquisite aroma filled the kitchen. It was sweet, yet at the same time, it...wasn't. It was hard to describe! But I supposed it could be called *kind of* sensual. In any case, every inhalation was heavenly.

I selected the tiniest crumb of mushroom and popped it into my mouth for a taste. Even that tiny piece flooded my mouth with a flavor I couldn't begin to capture in words.

"It tastes amazing," I murmured dreamily. Not the most descriptive statement, but it was all I could manage.

I wasn't alone either. The chefs nodded vigorously in agreement.

In the end, the white sauce went perfectly with the mushroom—that's what you get when you trust the expertise of professionals!

Everyone reconvened to enjoy the meal, by which I meant the chefs, my colleagues and the knights who had come with Jude and me, Johan, and even Albert, who Johan had invited. Drawn by the scent, my other colleagues flooded into the dining hall as well.

Even the smallest bit of the shadow mushroom was deliciously pungent, so we only had to sprinkle a smidgen on a serving and it did the job. We somehow had enough to let everyone get a taste, which was important to me.

(I feared that the day we didn't have enough of a new dish to go around would be the day we needed a lottery to determine who got to eat—and on that day, we would see bloodshed.)

In the end, though, I got to see everyone's utterly satisfied faces, which made me understand why this mushroom so consistently captivated people. I, too, was now a devotee. It had been so unimaginably delicious.

If possible, I hoped to eat it again someday, but I couldn't assume I'd ever get the chance. And using my Saint's powers to wish for something like that would be a little too self-interested, don't you think? Even so, I was tempted... What a good mushroom!

That Which Drives Women Wild

We KEPT AN HERB GARDEN next to the Research Institute of Medicinal Flora. The researchers all individually took care of their own plots.

One sunny day, I was busy tending my own plot when a shadow fell over me. The shadow held a parasol, so I instantly knew it wasn't one of my colleagues. Who could it be then? I turned around to find a familiar face. "Liz!"

"Hello, Sei." Liz smiled.

I couldn't hide my surprise. I mean, before that point, we had only ever met at the library.

Now that I think about it, didn't I invite her to see our garden way back when? Oh, gosh, that was the first time we met.

"Welcome!" I greeted her more properly. "Thanks for coming all this way."

"You told me I should come by and see the garden if I ever wished to, didn't you? So, here I am."

"I did, didn't I? How about we go inside the institute instead of standing around out here in the sun?"

So, we headed toward the institute. Although it was located next to the garden, it was still a short walk. But it wouldn't feel like any time at all if we chatted along the way.

"Oh, was there any specific plant you wanted to see? I can show you around if you'd like."

"I am indeed interested in the herbs you grow, but I have some more pressing questions to ask you about cosmetics."

"Cosmetics?"

"Yes. Do you remember the ones you made before? They worked marvelously well. However..."

As Liz trailed off, my cheek twitched. A while ago now, I had given Liz some cosmetics I'd made, and they had worked so well that they'd become popular with the young ladies at the academy. I'd received so many requests that I'd sold the recipe to a company in the city, which now made their own line. It would have been too difficult to fill all the requests I was getting on my own.

After the company started selling these cosmetics, Liz had gone to buy them there. However, after using the company's line, she discovered they weren't as effective as the kind I had made.

What did I mean by "effective"? Well, that had to do with why Liz had come to see me. I knew the answer to her question already: my fifty percent bonus curse. For some reason, anything I made, be it potions or food, was half again as effective as anything made by someone else. This curse extended to the cosmetics I concocted as well.

I had no doubt that Liz had come asking about something to do with the curse. But I wasn't sure if I should be honest about it. It seemed safest to ask Johan before I said anything.

I hated having to do it, but I would have to evade her question at first. Hopefully, I'd be able to tell her all about it someday.

When we arrived at the institute, I showed Liz to the drawing room. Since we handled confidential projects, I hesitated to lead her into the main workroom itself.

"I'll bring some tea. Do you like herbal varieties?" I asked.

"Quite. I adore them. Thank you."

"Great. I'll be right back."

I'd assumed Liz would be more accustomed to drinking black tea, but I didn't have such expensive blends on hand. However, the institute did keep some for high-ranking visitors. And not everyone liked herbal teas, so I asked her just in case.

I told Liz to wait and headed into the kitchen to make the tea. We always kept hot water available in our kitchen. Therefore, the tea was ready right away. After heating up the pot, I drained the water once and then filled it with new water and herbs. It would be done steeping by the time I got back to the drawing room.

I put the teapot, cups, and some cookies on a tray and headed back to find Liz gazing absentmindedly out the window.

"Sorry to have kept you waiting."

Liz smiled when I came into the room. Ahhh, she was just so *cute*. I felt all warm and fuzzy whenever she smiled like that. I placed a cup in front of her and poured the tea.

She inhaled the steam. "Oh? This aroma has so many different notes, but it smells lovely."

"Thanks. It's one of my own blends."

In Salutania, they largely drank herbal teas for medicinal purposes rather than for pleasure. As such, even when they purposefully blended herbs to make new teas, they prioritized what was healthy and didn't think much about the flavor or fragrance. Basically, I had yet to try a Salutanian herbal tea that tasted remotely good.

It was admittedly difficult to find a perfect match between herbs, so when Salutanians did make herbal teas, they typically only used one herb at a time. I myself had only recently started making my own blends. Today I had combined chamomile, rose, and rose hips. It was a recipe I remembered from Japan, and supposedly it was good for dry skin.

The moment I told Liz this, her eyes lit up. "Goodness, I knew that herbs had medicinal benefits, but I never imagined that might include skincare."

"You guys don't have any food you consider good for your skin?"

"Not at all. I've never heard of such a thing."

That made sense. Thinking back, Johan had listened with keen interest when I told him about cooking based on traditional Chinese medicine. To think that they didn't have anything like that here! Maybe they'd just never experimented with food in that way since they had potions?

"What about potions that are supposed to be good for your skin? Do you have anything like that?" I asked.

"Potions for skincare?!" Liz's eyes widened. Being at that young age, she was really interested in anything and everything that had to do with beauty care. "Do such potions really exist?"

"Not that I know of, but I've heard of something similar."

"Could you make it?"

"Hmm."

I was thinking of something called herbal cordials. They were sold in stores in modern day Japan, but they had once been made in homes. I was pretty sure they were easy to manufacture, too: you just had to boil herbs and sugar together in a pot. So yeah, if I had the ingredients, I could indeed make them.

When I told Liz this, she said, "I'd love to try it."

I couldn't get everything all together on the spot, so I told her I'd bring the finished product to her later at the library.

Three days after, I gave Liz the herbal cordial I had concocted.

The next day, she came to me smiling and exclaiming, even though we were in the library. "Sei! The cordial you gave me the other day was simply splendid!"

It was just the two of us in the library at that moment, but we would have earned all sorts of disapproving glances if anyone else had been there! Liz was normally so discreet, too, so if she had forgotten herself like this, the cordial must have been absurdly effective.

Then I got to see what she was so excited about with my own eyes. The cordial, which might as well have been called a potion, really did work.

Maybe it was because I was already using cosmetics I had made myself, but I hadn't thought there was much of a change when I tried it myself. However, when I had one of the other researchers try it out, the change was tremendous. He had been neglecting his skin because of research lately, but the second he drank the cordial, his skin got all smooth and shiny. Even his complexion improved, giving a rosy color to his lips and cheeks.

The change was so dramatic that the other researchers stopped what they were doing to gape.

Yeahhh, this definitely had something to do with my fifty percent bonus curse. However, I wasn't sure if cordials drew from my Pharmaceuticals skill or Cooking skill, which was why I wasn't sure whether I should classify them as potions per se. They weren't really a kind of medicine. Maybe more of a vitamin drink?

After that, Liz's persistence overcame my reservations, and I sold the cordial recipe to the company in the city as well.

Beauty products sure drive women wild. I had never seen Liz so worked up before.

That reminded me—she completely forgot about the cosmetics question she had originally come to ask, but I had a feeling she'd come back around to it later.

In the meantime, I'd have to ask Johan for advice on how to handle an overenthusiastic young woman.

Report

IKNOCKED ON THE DOOR and got permission to enter, so I entered the room to meet my doom. I pushed a tea cart with a pot of herbal tea and teacups on it before me.

Johan chuckled humorlessly as I approached his desk. "You seem prepared."

"I thought we might be talking a while."

"Do we have that much to discuss?"

All I could do was let out a strained laugh as Johan hung his head. Although he had heard a bit about what my transgressions were already, he hadn't thought it would warrant a full tea service. Johan doubtless suspected that the length of this talk would directly correlate to the amount of time he'd have to devote to cleaning up my mess. Unfortunately, I was about to confirm his suspicions.

I'm sorry!

Today, I had come to Johan's office to debrief him on my trip to Klausner's Domain. Albert had already told him about how I purged the black swamp. Albert had also told him there were some other things he needed to hear about, which was why I had been summoned today.

I poured the tea and placed the cups on the table. Johan then came over to sit on one of the two sofas facing each other. His eyes softened when he spied the pound cake the chefs had given me. It wasn't much, just enough to make a good snack before lunch.

As soon as I sat down, Johan jumped to the main subject. "So? Just how much do you have to confess, then?"

"Well..."

Quite a bit, even just off the top of my head. Despite the steps I'd taken to fly under the radar, I'd cooked for Lord Klausner and suspected I had kind of overdone it with the potion making. Also, I definitely had to tell Johan about the potion recipes I had learned at the brewery and about the rare herbs that needed blessings to grow properly.

I counted these events off on my fingers, each of which made Johan's expression gradually stiffen more and more.

"You must be kidding me," he moaned.

"Which would you like first, the good news or the bad news? Maybe the bad news?"

He hung his head again. "There's bad news, too?"

"You didn't hear from Lord Hawke?"

"I heard that you'd have some things to tell me, but no details."

Eep. He wasn't the least bit prepared. I winced, but I figured I might as well get it over with. After I finished, Johan looked weary. It made me feel super guilty, especially when I thought of how hard he had to work to smooth things over after I charged through.

"Um, Johan?"

"Is that all?" he asked weakly.

"Yes, for the bad news."

His head continued to hang, held in his hands. I drained my cup of herbal tea and glanced away. Hey—was he mumbling?

"Johan?" He was speaking so quietly I couldn't make it out.

"Did you cook something new while you were there?"

"Ah, yes."

"Can you make it here?"

"Oh, sure, if I can get the ingredients."

Johan raised his head a little and looked at me reproachfully.

Yeah, yeah, I get it! The ingredients weren't all that unusual, so it probably wouldn't take too long to round them all up. I would ask the chef later.

As I nodded in confirmation, Johan's expression grew less demoralized than lightly tired, and he straightened. "So, now for the good news?"

"Uh, I think so," I replied with a strained smile, which made his mouth twitch. *I mean, probably the rest won't give him any further headaches. It's all just about herbs, after all.*

And indeed, when I described the herbs we would now be able to cultivate with blessings, his expression lit up. He did work at the research institute, after all. He was reliably invested in anything to do with herbs and potions.

"Of *course* there would be so much to learn at a place known as the alchemist's holy land."

"Yeah, I definitely learned a lot."

"This business about the Saint-related growing conditions for certain herbs—that's especially interesting."

"It is! It was such a lucky coincidence that I learned about that."

"It's a bit problematic that the alchemists of Klausner's Domain know about it, but you made sure that they'll keep quiet, right?"

"Mm-hmm."

"Good. I suppose the palace will have to send directions to Lord Klausner to ensure he doesn't disclose this information either."

"I'm really sorry about that." I bowed in apology.

Johan sighed before he said, "Well, it's fine."

I couldn't tell him the whole truth, so I apologized to him again in my mind.

I had to pretend to be the one who had discovered how to grow herbs with blessings using the Saint's power. Corinna had suggested this, actually. It had been her condition for allowing me to grow the same herbs at the institute. After all, Lord Klausner and Corinna didn't want anyone to learn the truth about the Great Alchemist's diary. Having me take credit for discovering the technique helped them cover their tracks. More than anything, they were grateful that they would once more be able to grow those valuable herbs and thereby save their domain's economy.

I still felt phenomenally guilty whenever I thought of taking credit away from the person who had actually developed the technique, but I was too captivated by the opportunity to grow new herbs at the institute. *I'm really sorry, Great Alchemist...*

"I suppose that gives me plenty to do for the time

being, but at least there are some things I'll be looking forward to as well."

"Y-yeah... I'm sorry, but could I ask you to help me with growing those rare herbs?"

Johan beamed. "Of course."

He really did have the same passion for herbs that I did.

Now that I was done with that report, we were able to start happily discussing what was to come.

Afterword

Hᴇʟʟᴏ, ᴛʜɪs ɪs Yuka Tachibana. Thank you for buying *The Saint's Magic Power is Omnipotent*, Volume Four.

It's thanks to you that this story made it so far. I was pretty surprised that I managed to continue the story this long. I'd like to thank you all for always cheering me on. As usual, Volume Three ended on a cliffhanger, so I wanted to get this book out as soon as possible. I'm relieved I managed to make it within a year.

I'd also like to thank my editor, W from Kadokawa Books, for this volume. He made every effort to adjust the schedule for me on this book. I'm always causing trouble for other people in addition to W, so I apologize for that. Thank you for everything. One of these days, I'll be able to follow the original schedule to the letter...

So, did you all enjoy this volume? From this point on there will be some spoilers, so please make sure to read the main story first.

When writing this afterword, I looked back at the one I wrote for Volume Three and noticed I had written that I wanted to develop Sei's relationship with Albert. Now looking back at this volume, I'm not sure if I can say there's been any development at all. I didn't have any specific plans, but how did this happen? There's just not much happening between them, since I'm trying to write the story while balancing it against Sei's low level in love. She really only thinks about herbs and work. This series was supposed to be romantic, so I'd like Sei to put a little more effort in. Huh? I should shift the responsibility to Albert instead? ...Sorry, Albert.

I feel like the grand magus played a bigger role than Albert did. Sei used her powers more often in this volume, so perhaps that meant Yuri would inevitably appear more often, given his obsession with magic, but I don't think he was around *too* much. Yuri's an easy character to write, or perhaps I should say he writes himself, so I realized that unless I'm careful, he might start taking over. Some other characters are similarly easy to write, but Albert isn't one of them, so that might be why there's still such little development in their relationship (and a certain someone else's problem).

Even so, due to various circumstances (mostly because of me), the Klausner's Domain arc stretched over two volumes. However, we finally got the word "muscle" to show up in the bibliographic information. My editor wrote it, and I burst out laughing when he sent it over text message for me to check. Thank you for the great write-up, W. I had personally been thinking of these two volumes as the muscle volumes, so maybe I should've gone a bit crazier with it? I was worried that I'd lose readers by inserting too many of my own interests, but I think I want to add more muscles here and there from now on.

I also want there to be a bit more romance in Volume Five. And more of the easy life! I want to go back to an easy life! I realized nothing ever happens between Sei and Albert when I push Sei's job as the Saint too much! Sei really is such a workaholic in the way she always chooses work over romance. Admittedly, she'd deny that. And probably tell me to shut it because I'm the one making her work.

Yasuyuki Syuri did the art for this volume, too. Thank you for more wonderful illustrations. Personally, I was glad to see so many of Sei this time. She's just so cute... And Aira's on the cover, too, so there's lots of girls, which makes me happy. And also, Yuri! I like the picture of Yuri staring at Sei. He has a really nice smile on his face (lol).

If I had to choose a favorite from all of the pictures in this volume, it would be that one—that's just how much I like it. I want to see more illustrations of Sei, so I'm going to keep working hard to write more volumes.

Thankfully, the manga is still going, too. It's doing quite well. Starting with Fujiazuki-sensei, I'd like to say thank you to everyone involved. While I wrote the original story, I found myself unconsciously drawn into it whenever I had to check the scripts and kept forgetting what I was supposed to be doing. Recently, I've been reading it once for pleasure and then making a second pass to actually do my checks. The chibi characters are so cute and bring a smile to my face every time I see them.

You can read the wonderful manga version at ComicWalker, pixiv Comic, and Nico Nico Seiga*. You can read part of it for free, so please do so if you're interested. The latest chapter has a scene where Sei and Albert are flirting, so you can replenish your thirst for romance by reading the manga instead.

Lastly, thank you for reading up until this point. I'm going to work as hard as I can to get Volume Five into your hands as soon as possible. I hope to see you again soon.

Look for it in English, also from Seven Seas!

SHORT STORY COLLECTION
First Appearances